FAIR PLAY

RONALD SIEBERT

TABLE OF CONTENTS

One...1

Two..4

Three..7

Four..10

Five..14

Six...19

Seven...24

Eight...29

Nine..32

Ten...35

Eleven..38

Twelve..41

Thirteen..46

Fourteen..50

Fifteen...56

Sixteen...59

Seventeen...64

Eighteen..67

Nineteen..72

Twenty..75

Twenty-One..78

Twenty-Two..83

Twenty-Three..89

Twenty-Four...92

Twenty-Five...96

Twenty-Six 99

Twenty-Seven 102

Twenty-Eight 107

Twenty-Nine 113

Thirty 116

Thirty-One 119

Thirty-Two 122

Thirty-Three 128

Thirty-Four 131

Thirty-Five 135

Thirty-Six 140

Thirty-Seven 146

Thirty-Eight 149

Thirty-Nine 151

Forty 154

Forty-One 159

Forty-Two 163

Forty-Three 169

Forty-Four 175

Forty-Five 182

Forty-Six..185

Forty-Seven..188

Forty-Eight 191

Forty-Nine 194

Fifty..196

Fifty-One 198

Fifty-Two 203

Fifty-Three...206

Fifty-Four 211

Fifty-Five 216

Fifty-Six 218

Fifty-Seven 221

Fifty-Eight 225

Fifty-Nine 230

Sixty 236

Sixty-One 243

Sixty-Two 248

Sixty-Three 252

Sixty-Four 257

Sixty-Five 261

Sixty-Six 264

Sixty-Seven 267

Sixty-Eight 270

Sixty-Nine 274

ONE

BRUCE

As the train pulled into the station, I couldn't help but rejoice. I will be feeling the blessed sun for a change. This damn coach has been so cold, I thinking about asking for a blanket. Now, as the train neared the station, I was in a hurry to get off. Looking out the window and seeing the sun, I knew it wouldn't be long before I could get warm again.

To be sure I had a head start for getting off, I left my seat long before the train came to a full stop. Quickly making my way to where all the baggage was stored, I had to dig the bag out. Once I had my baggage in hand, I was ready for an easy departure.

A sudden movement of people made me stand off to the side to let them pass. I'm about to give up my position by the hatch. By the way everyone was moving, I knew I only had a short wait until the train came to a full stop.

Hearing the screech of the brakes and feeling the surge of the train braking, I braced myself against the wall to maintain my balance. Once the train came to its jarring stop, the conductor would open the hatch and step out. Once the conductor was out, he had to put the step in place before we could exit.

The moment the hatch opened, a wave of hot, humid air flooded the train. It felt as if we were entering a blast furnace. Now with the step down, I made my exit. Hitting the pavement, I threw my sea bag over my shoulder and started for the terminal. That first step seemed like a long way down and jarred me.

Now, on the hot pavement, the temperature and humidity seemed to rise drastically. Inside the train, the temperature felt like sixty degrees. Outside, the temperature was the complete opposite. Going from sixty degrees to the upper nineties was a shock to the system.

Now, not only was the heat in the air extreme, but the heat of the pavement quickly soaked through the soles of my shoes, making me want to move quicker. The longer I was in this heat and humidity, it was almost unbearable.

I hadn't moved more than twenty feet when sweat began to pour down my forehead and into my eyes. Before I got to the terminal, the shirt on my back was completely soaked with sweat and was sticking to my skin.

Looking ahead, it seemed to be a long way to the depot building. In my estimation, the distance, at fifty yards or more.

Already feeling the heat through the soles of my shoes, I knew it was going to be a long day. Getting to the terminal was the easy part; I still had to get to the main road, where I had to hitch a ride.

As hot and humid as it is, the walk from the terminal to the main drag, in this heat it was going to sap my strength. I could only hope I didn't have too long a wait to catch a ride. Being I was in my summer uniform, it would help a little. I was hoping my uniform might help for a quicker ride.

Each step I took made my sea bag seem to gain weight. I moved as quickly as I could. When I reached the terminal, I was going to take a break and sit on one of those hard benches to gain some strength. It had been a really short distance to the terminal, but the weight and the heat made the time seem like hours.

Sitting on the hard wooden bench wasn't what anyone would call comfortable, but at least it was a seat, and it was a lot cooler than being outside.   Once I felt somewhat cooler, I stood, picked up my seabag, and made my way to the entrance.

Getting to the main road, I had to walk at least ten blocks. Knowing the walk, in this heat, was going to make me feel extremely uncomfortable, I forced myself to take the first step. Leave to coolness of the building was depressing. Just those few minutes of cool temperature really were not enough, but what little I had felt was better than nothing.

Stepping into the heat again was a shock. Gritting my teeth, I began the long trek to the main road. After walking just five of the ten blocks, I felt wilted. Turning the corner and looking straight ahead, and knowing I had another five more blocks to go, I sagged.

Finally reaching the main road, I saw what looked like a shady spot under a huge Oak tree, not too far away. I knew it wasn't going to be much cooler, but at least I would be out of the sun.

Each step he took was agonizing to him. For a while, he didn't think he would ever get there. Between the humidity and the hot sun bearing down on me, I felt extremely exhausted. Lucky for me, this huge Oak had large overhanging branches.

TWO

BRUCE

Reaching the huge Oak tree, I dropped my sea bag. No longer caring how dirty I got, I sagged to the ground, using the tree as a backrest. After somewhat composing myself, he quickly swiped the sweat from my eyes.

Dreading the thought of standing in that hot sun again, didn't enthuse me very much. Also knowing I wouldn't be getting a ride sitting here in the shade, I forced myself to my hot, tired feet.

There was one small spot in the shade I could still use. It was better than standing in the open sun. Even standing in the shade, I frequently had to take off my hat to wipe my brow.

Feeling very tired and uncomfortable in my uniform, I sighed. Even standing in the shade, blocking the sun, wasn't any help as far as getting a ride. Sticking out his thumb, I kept hoping I wouldn't have to wait too long to catch a ride. A hot breeze blowing through the area was beginning to irritate me. This little bit of shade wasn't making mt feel any cooler.

Standing where I was, I began thinking of an alternative. As much as I dreaded getting into the sun, I knew standing here, in this shade, wasn't going to get mee a ride. If moving into the sun would improve my chances of catching a ride, then I guess I will do it.

Just after moving into the sun, luck seemed to be on my side. A few moments later, a White Cadillac Convertible, with its top down,

pulled over to the side of the road. I didn't care if the top was down.
I would at least have a seat and be moving.

As he moved toward the waiting vehicle, I couldn't help notice the
car was being driven by an older woman. She had stopped for me, a few
feet down the road, but at least she stopped. Instead of backing up for
me, the woman turned in her seat and shouted at me.

"Just throw your bag in the backseat," she hollered to me.

"Thanks," I uttered.

Throwing my bag carefully into the back seat, I grasped the door
handle, which turned out to be a mistake. The sun had made the handle
extremely hot.

"Damn," I uttered.

Pulling his hand away, I thought I had singed my hand.

"Where are you headed, sailor?" she asked.

"Madison," I told her.

"Perfect, that is the way I am headed," she said in a cheerful voice.

"Hop in."

Not wanting to kick a gift horse in the mouth, even though I would
still be still sitting in the sun, I reached for the door again. Ignoring the
pain, I pulled the handle a second time. This time, the door opened.

As I slid into the front seat beside the woman, the view I got was
fantastic. The way the woman's skirt was showing her legs and crotch
almost made me forget the heat. The heat from the leather seats singed
the cheeks of my ass, through my pants.

"Sorry about the hot seats," she laughed.

As soon as I was seated and buckled in, the woman extended her
small, dainty hand to me. Taking her hand, I couldn't help but let my
eyes take in the sight a little more. I couldn't help but like what I was
seeing. Never mind, the woman might be a little older than I was.

Actually, she was a very beautiful woman, and it seemed she didn't mind showing what she had.

She was wearing a short white skirt. The way she was wearing the skirt, she was showed off a beautiful pair of legs. Forcing my eyes up to look into hers, they passed by what was a loose-fitting blouse. The blouse was a white blouse, which matched her shorts. That look gave her a very sexy look.

Lastly, I saw her smile. It was coming from a beautiful face. All these looks made me forget the heat pouring down. The only thing melting at this moment was his lonely heart.

My first thought was, some lucky guy had to be bedding down this incredible creature. He really had to be enjoying himself. As she pulled into traffic, I found it very difficult to keep my eyes from wandering. The woman had incredibly beautiful legs.

As she drove, she continued to stare at the road. Letting my gaze travel upward to that loose-fitting blouse, I saw what looked to be small breasts. She wore her pretty, light red hair, tied in a ponytail, to keep it from snarling in the wind. With her hair up, it showed her long, slender neck. My guess about her age would be somewhere in her late twenties, maybe early thirties.

Caught staring at her, she smiled.

"Do you like what you see?" she asked.

"Any fool would," I told her.

THREE

BRUCE

Then, giving me another quick glance, she said, "My name is Lana Collins."

"It is nice to meet you, Lana Collins, I'm Bruce."

"Do you have a last name, Bruce?"

"I'm sorry. Yes. It is Benson, I'm Bruce Benson."

"Are you visiting your parents, Bruce Benson?" she asked.

"Yes, I am Lana Collins."

"How long will you be home?"

"I'll be here for three weeks."

"Where are you stationed?"

"A place called Port Hueneme, California."

"What do you do there?"

"I'm a draftsman in the Navy Seabees."

"Oh, I've never met a Seabee before. What is a Seabee?"

Turning in my seat to face her, I returned her smile.

"We do construction, such as building bases, bridges, towers and roads."

"That sounds interesting," she said.

Unable to stop my eyes from taking in her beauty, I knew I had. She smiled and chuckled.

Wanting to keep the conversation going, he asked, "What do you do for a living?"

"I'm a hairdresser," she said.

"Where do you live?" I asked.

"For the summer, I live in Clinton."

"Oh, I guess that makes us nearly neighbors then."

"For three weeks anyway," she said.

"I want to thank you for the ride," I said softly.

"Believe me, it is my pleasure," she said

Not knowing what else to talk about, other than what I do, we rode in silence for a while.

Then out of the blue, she asked, "Are you hungry?"

"Yes."

"How would you like to stop for lunch?"

"I would, if I can buy," I told her.

"Oh no," she said, "You are my treat."

A few miles further, Lana turned down a quiet street. The branches of the huge Oak trees growing along the road gave the appearance of driving beneath a canopy. At the end of the street, she pulled into a small café. We were sitting at the edge of the sound, with the sound of waves striking the pier.

"Wait," I said quickly.

To my surprise, Lana remained seated. She wanted to see what I had in mind. Getting out of my seat, I moved quickly around the car to her side.   Opening her door, I offered my hand. I could hardly wait for her to extract her beautiful body from the car.

Knowing I had an imposing figure, standing six feet three and weighing two hundred twenty pounds, I absolutely wanted to show her my good side.

With a smile, she took my hand.   As she was coming to a stand, I got another sweet view of her panties.   For some reason, she opened her legs to slide out. It wasn't the most graceful move, but I was happy she did it.   She sure had one sexy body for a woman her age.

As we approached the cafe door, Lana looked up at me and gave me a warm smile.   Wanting to make a nice appearance for her, I took the time to open the cafe door for her.   Stepping aside, I let her enter first. As she passed me, I caught a good whiff of her perfume.

Stopping the moment she entered, Lana waited for me to follow. Inside, I stepped beside her.   Placing my hand in the small of her back, I led her to the podium to wait for a waitress.

As we were waiting, I couldn't get over how absolutely stunning Lana was. When the waitress appeared, with menus in her hand, she motioned for us to follow her. She led us to a booth overlooking the water.

Following Lana closely with my eyes, I couldn't help admire the movement of her tight little butt with each step she took.   When we neared the table, I managed to beat her to her chair.   Pulling out her chair, I waited until she was comfortable before pushing her chair in. Satisfied she was comfortable, I strutted to the other side of the table, taking a seat facing her.

"You are a real gentleman," she whispered.

"I always try making beautiful women comfortable."

"I like you already," she said.

FOUR

LANA

I had just left the conference building. It wasn't very late, so having some free time, to spend on myself, I decided to spend a couple of hours at the beach. Heading toward the beach, I was going to the one place I loved, where I could relax.

If there was one place on this earth where I could assess what I was doing with my life, it would be the beach. Knowing there were some changes to be made and knowing I had to have the time and space to think, the beach was the place.

Taking the elevator to the garage, where I left my car, I found it quiet and peaceful. Leaving the elevator, I walked slowly to my car. The first thing I did was put the top down. I knew it was going to be hot, but while the car was moving, it felt cool. Besides, I like the feel of the sun on my skin.

Before driving, to keep her hair from snarling, while the motor ran, I put her hair in a ponytail. With my top down and my hair set to stop the snarls, I drove into the hot sun. It wasn't long after I drove out of my parking space, I found the main road. Driving another two blocks, I turned the corner.

Now headed in the direction of the beach, she was able to let her mind rest. While enjoying the wind blowing through my hair, out of the corner of my eye, I saw him. I couldn't believe my eyes. Standing just off the road was this handsome young man in a naval uniform. He was thumbing a ride. Liking what I saw, I made a quick decision. With not enough time to stop by him, when I pulled over to the side of the road, I found I was a little past the place he was standing.

Feeling lonely and forgotten, my mind quickly jumped to the subject of sex. Sadly, sex was something I couldn't get enough of and in reality, didn't get enough of. In fact, it has been over two months since the last time my husband touched me. That one time, or should I say, the last few times, were not satisfying.

Eric, my husband of nineteen years, is always traveling for his work. When he does come home, usually on the weekends, he hardly looks at me, let alone touches me. His inattention was making me think Eric was having an affair with someone else.

I was having those lonesome feelings and a dire need for masculine attention. Those feelings and needs were enough for me to pull over for the guy. Once at the side of the road, I turned in my seat to see where he was. Seeing him, I shouted at him.

He was carrying some kind of bag. When he did, I heard him grumble about the hot door handle.

"Where are you headed?" I asked him.

"Madison," he told me.

Right away, her heart began beating wildly.

"Perfect, that is where I am headed," I told him, "Just throw your bag in the back seat and hop in."

"Thanks," he said.

Seeing how easily the young man threw that big bag over his shoulder made me yearn to feel those big, strong arms around me. The closer the guy got to her car, the more I yearned to know him better. There were those warning signs, but I had long forgotten them and didn't care.

Sexual satisfaction was all I could think about. God, what a hunk the young man is. Then she told herself, he looks so young. Because I liked the sound of his voice, I let all the warning signs pass me by. As he easily placed his bag in the back seat, I admired his strength.

When he reached to open the door a second time, I could see the look on his face, the handle had to be very hot. Nevertheless, ignoring the pain, he opened the door and slid in. His uniform was so tight, it didn't hide any of the muscle action hidden beneath his clothes.

As he slid into the car, I could feel his eyes fasten on me. His look gave me a thrill. I haven't had those feelings in a long time. The way and direction of his eyes looked at me quickly turned me on. It was obvious he liked what he was seeing. This was the perfect time for me to be wearing my white shorts and loose-fitting white blouse.

For encouragement, I gave him a warm smile. Another thing that turned me on was the way his eyes kept staring at my legs. That was a good sign.

It wasn't long after he was seated and buckled up, I drove away. I could still feel his eyes traveling from my legs upward, toward my breasts and face. Even though my breasts are small, I was sorry I wore such a loose blouse.

The blouse was pretty and appropriate for what I had to do, but the blouse did hid the small curves of my breasts. Wearing a ponytail, at least gave him a view of my long neck, which I was proud of, and knew that most men liked a long neck.

When I caught him staring at me again, I smiled. Then, quickly glancing at him, I said, "My name is Lana Collins."

Needing and wanting to touch him, I extended my hand to him. The strength of his grip was another turn on which made me swoon inside.

Needing to learn more about this young man, I began questioning him.

"It is nice to meet you, Lana, I'm Bruce."

"Do you have a last name, Bruce?"

"I'm sorry. Yes. It is Benson."

After learning his name and what he did in the military, I knew I had to get to know this young man a lot better.   I can overlook how much younger he is than I am.   When he shifted in his seat to face me, I knew I had his full attention.

Then I noticed the bulge in his uniform.   It wasn't hard and was already big.   God, he was young, but oh so handsome.   Liking the way his eyes studied me and what he had in his pants, I couldn't help but smile to give him a little encouragement.

"Do you like what you see?" I asked.

"I'd be a fool if I didn't," he answered.

It was then that I made up my mind.   I wanted more time with this young man.   Making a quick decision, I asked, "Are you hungry?"

"Yes."

"I know the perfect place," I told him.

A few miles up the road, I turned down a quiet street.   It was quaint. Long branches of the huge Oak trees, on each side of the street, gave off the appearance of riding beneath a canopy.   At the end of the street, I pulled into a small cafe.   The cafe sat by the wharf, at the edge of the sound, where people liked to wander.

"Wait," he told me.

Remaining seated, I watched him quickly getting out of the car, then rush around to open my door.   Wow, was he always this way, or is he just trying to impress me?   So far, I liked everything about him.   His height had to be over six foot, and his weight was somewhere around two hundred to two hundred fifty pounds.   It looked to be all muscle.

When he opened my door and extended his hand, I quickly took it. With my hand in his, I allowed him to help me out of the car.   God, he was strong. Knowing this was my chance, I nonchalantly spread my legs a little for a better view.

FIVE

LANA

When he pulled me up, I didn't let go of his hand. Standing next to him was the first time I realized how tall and big he really was. The top of my head barely reached his armpit. Stepping aside, I let him close the door and lock it.

After locking the car, he turned back toward me. When he looked at me with those big blue eyes, I just wanted to melt. I couldn't help but swoon inside. To make matters worse, when he placed his hand on the small of my back, I let him gently lead me into the restaurant, and I did so on wobbly knees.

I haven't felt this much like a woman in a long time. The beat of my heart was pumping wildly. I wondered if everyone around us could hear it. Daring a glance up at him, when I saw him looking at me, all I could give him was a genuinely warm smile.

At the entrance, he opened the cafe door. Letting me enter first. Passing as close to him as I could without touching him, I hoped he would catch a whiff of my favorite perfume.

Stepping inside, I waited for him to enter. As I assume, he placed his hand on my back, leading me to the podium, where an old, heavy and cranky waitress was waiting for us at our table.

Knowing Bruce was following me, I did all I could to move my hips and walk as sexily as I could. At the table, the waitress stepped aside to let us be seated. Again, Bruce surprised me when he pulled out my chair.

It wasn't until I was comfortably seated that I pushed my chair beneath the table. Once I was settled, he casually walked to the other side, where he sat facing me.

"Could you give us five?" I asked the waitress.

"Yes, ma'am," she said and walked away.

Once the waitress was gone, I gave Bruce a sexy gaze before giving him another very warm smile.

"How old are you, Bruce?"

Seeing him hesitate, I thought he was going to lie. My guess, he was about twenty-five or six.

"I'm twenty-one."

Holly crap, I thought. That would make him thirteen years younger than me. Still, wanting what I originally wanted from him and liking his looks, I was willing to overlook the age difference. Besides, it suddenly felt exciting to perhaps be bedding with a younger man.

"Tell me more about yourself," I said.

Since I was already into this venture, with both feet, why not continue? From the physical look of him, I might really enjoy myself. It isn't every day, a woman thirteen years older than the man would have a chance like this.

Staring into his eyes, I did wonder about this situation. How badly did I want this? Was I really willing to get into this affair? The more I talked with him, the more comfortable I felt being with him. This was a strange thing for me to be doing. We had just met each other for the first time, and yet I'm wild for him.

When he asked my age, I hesitated for just a moment. Since he told me the truth about his age, I decided not to lie. Besides, I wanted to see his reaction when I gave him my age.

"I'm thirty-four. Does our age difference bother you?"

"Not at all," he said, "you don't look that age."

"How old did you think I was?"

"Late twenties," he said.

"I'll take that as a compliment."

Then, the question about my children came up.   To be on the safe side, I didn't want to mention their names.   I knew he saw the rings on my finger, so he knew I was married.   So, to be truthful, I told him how I felt and why.

After our little discussion, I was afraid to say anything else, so I ate in silence.   Even through our silence, I couldn't help but stare into his eyes. Once lunch was over, I didn't move; I was afraid to.   I wanted to see if Bruce would help me from my seat.

He didn't disappoint me.   Now came the difficult part.   Not knowing how else to give him money for the food, when I took his hand, I placed the money in his palm.   He never flinched, but he did take the time to throw a tip on the table.

Leaving the table, I latched on to him again, never wanting to let go of his hand.   At the register, the cashier looked at us.   His expression made me throw a loving practical joke at Bruce's expense.   I wanted to see both the guy's reaction, while I lovingly hung on to his arm.

"It's time for you to take me home, honey," she teased, "It is time you make me feel like your wife again."

That comment made the cashier chuckle.

"I guess I know where you are going," the guy said.

To my surprise, Bruce went along with me.

"We could have gone straight home instead of stopping here."

"You said you were hungry," I said.

"You didn't me a chance to say what I was hungry for," he said.

"Well, pay the man, so we can get home."

As I expected he would, when we reached the car, Bruce opened the car door for me.   Like the gentleman he seemed to be, he waited until I was settled before going to his side.

"You shouldn't tease a guy like that," he said, sliding into his seat.

"Who says I was teasing?" I commented.

"If you weren't teasing, please don't waste any more time getting us where you want to take me."

Starting the car, she giggled and drove away.

"I'm glad to know you are in a hurry too," I told him.

Suddenly, my cell phone rang.

"Oh shit," I grumbled.

I knew right away who the call was from, and it irritated me.   I was hoping to have a late afternoon of fantastic sex.   Pushing a button on the dashboard, my phone came to life.
"Hello, dear," I said.

"Where are you, Mom?"

"I'm on my way home," I told her.

Turning off my phone, I let off a deep sigh.

"I'm sorry," I said, "I was hoping to have a little more time with you alone."

"Don't be sorry, there will be other times, I hope," he said

"You had better believe there will be other times," I cried, "Now that I have your number, I will be calling."

When I neared Madison, I asked, "Where would you want me to drop you off?"

"You can drop me off by the restaurant outside the park."

When I pulled over and stopped, I couldn't help myself.   Before Bruce could get out of the car, I quickly moved into his arms for a kiss. Giving him a kiss, he wouldn't forget, I grabbed his crotch.   That was when I received the biggest surprise.

"That kiss is my promise to you.   I will be calling," I panted, "What I just felt is going to keep me yearning for you, until we are together again."

Six

BRUCE

ow that we were seated, the waitress handed us menus and poured water.

"Give us five," Lana told the waitress.

"Yes, Ma'am," the waitress said.

With the waitress gone, Lana gave me another very warm smile.

"How old are you, Bruce?"

The question stopped me. Not wanting to lie, I answered her correctly.

"I'm twenty-one," I uttered.

"Are you engaged or married?"

"Neither," I said, "But I did just break up with the girl I was living with, just before coming home."

"Could I ask what happened?"

"She told me she didn't like the fact I was gone nine months every year."

"Well, I sort of understand where she is coming from."

"And why is that?"

"My husband is never home either. Or, I should say, he only comes home on weekends. He says, his job takes him traveling, all over the place."

"I see the ring on your finger. He must make good money."

"He does, as do I. I in my own business."

"Do you have any children?" I asked.

"Yes, I have two daughters," she hesitated, "My oldest is fourteen and my youngest is eleven."

Noticing she never mentioned the daughter's names, nor did she mention her husband's name, I let it go. It got me thinking. Her oldest daughter would be seven years younger than me, and the other would be ten. Figuring Lana didn't give me any information, I had to assume she didn't want me to know.

"Where are the girls now?" I asked.

"They had better be in school," Lana said.

"If you don't mind me asking, where were you coming from when you picked me up?"

"I was at a hairdresser's conference, in New Haven," she said.

"Then, I imagine you are in a hurry to get home to them."

"Not really," she said, "The woman next door watches the girls until I get home. I never know when I have to work overtime."

"Are we ready?" the waitress asked, returning.

"Yes," Lana said.

Handing the waitress her menu, "I'll have a crab salad."

"And you, sir."

"I'd like a club sandwich," I told the waitress, giving her my menu.

"Will that be enough for you, honey?" Lana smirked.

Not expecting the words Lana said, I tried not to feel surprised. Was she trying to embarrass me, or did she love playing jokes? Not giving her the edge, I went along with her.

"I'm just in a hurry to get home. It has been a while, dear."

With a grin, Lana turned to the waitress and said, "My husband just came home on leave."

"Lucky you," the waitress snarled, "I don't have a husband."

With a huff, the waitress left to place their order.

"I hope you don't mind me saying that," Lana said, "I just couldn't resist."

"I'm flattered," I told her.

"The waitress must be thinking, what is that old biddy doing with that sexy young man."

"I don't think so." I said, "You look younger than your actual age, which I figure is late twenties, or real early thirties."

"Thank you," she whispered, I'm actually thirty-four."

"Then, your husband is a lucky guy."

"He doesn't seem to think so," she said.

"Why do you say that?"

"I think the bastard is cheating on me."

"You have to be kidding," I gasped.

Wanting to see her reaction, I was willing to play her game.

"If you were my wife, I'd make sure to keep you happy, if you know what I mean."

Chuckling, Lana said, "I know what you mean. I shouldn't say this, but... I'm a very lonesome woman.   Needing a real man's companionship, even if it is for a short time.   That was one of the reasons I wanted to take you to lunch."

"One of the reasons?" I asked, "What is the other reason?"

"Would you consider letting me take you to dinner sometime?"

"I would love to go out with you," I said, returning her smile, "but will your daughters or husband understand?"

"You don't have to worry about them," Lana whispered, "I can always come up with a good excuse."

Then, after some hesitation, she said, "I usually go out one night a week anyway."

"If I'm not being too nosy, what do you do?"

"Would it be too presumptuous of me to ask you for a phone number, where I can reach you?"

"Do you have a pen?" I asked.

Reaching into her purse, Lana handed me a pen and a card.

"This is my cellphone number," I told her.

Handing the card back to her, I stared longingly into her eyes.

I held the card tightly as she tried to snatch it.   When she looked at me, I released my hold.

"Thanks," she said.

Sticking the card back into her purse, she finished the food silently. Neither of us could help but stare at the other from across the table. With lunch over, Lana remained seated, waiting for me to pull her chair away from the table.

After doing so, I again gave her my hand.   Standing, Lana grasped my hand more tightly.   To my surprise, she had handed me the money for lunch.

"I like it when the man does the paying," she said.

Accepting the money, I took out my wallet to at least place a tip on the table.   Turning my attention back to Lana, she made sure her hand was secured in mine.   As I led her across the room to the cashier, she followed like the dutiful wife.

As we walked away from the table, Lana hung tightly onto my hand, giving everyone the impression, we were really married.   At the cashier, Lana did it again.

"It's time to get me home, honey," she teased, "It has been a long time since the last time we saw each other."

The cashier chuckled.

"I guess I know where the two of you are going," the guy said.

SEVEN

BRUCE

In the three weeks since I broke up with Judy, I have remained celibate. For some reason, just Lana's words were enough to make me hard. Going along with her teasing, I patted her softly on the ass, as we walked away.

Then, wrapping my arm around her waist, I led her outside. Always wanting to be a gentleman, once outside, I opened the driver's door for her again. When I was sure she was comfortable, I took my time getting to my side of the car. Sliding into my seat, I turned to look at her.

"You shouldn't tease a guy like this," I told her.

"Who says I was teasing?" Lana commented.

Well, if you weren't teasing, why in the hell are you wasting so much time getting us to where you want to take me?"

Without saying a word, Lana started the car and drove off.

"I'm glad to see you are in a hurry too," she said.

No sooner had they left the parking lot when her cell phone rang.

"Oh shit," she said.

Pushing a button on the dashboard, her phone came to life. "Hello, dear, Lana said.

"Where are you, Mom?"

"I'm on my way," Lana told her.

Turning off her phone, Lana said, "I'm sorry. I was hoping we had a little more time to be alone."

"Don't be sorry," I told her ", Maybe there will be another time like this."

"You had better believe there will be other times," Lana said, "Now that I have your number, I will be calling."

A little further up the road, Lana asked in a dejected voice, "Where would you want me to drop you off?"

"You can drop me off at the restaurant, just outside the park."

Pulling up at the corner, Lana instantly moved against me to give me a lip lock I would never forget. During the kiss, Lana deftly groped my crotch.

"This is my promise to you that I will be calling," she moaned. "What I just felt will keep me yearning until we are together again."

Before I could get out of the car, she hungrily kissed me again. With that last kiss, I shoved my tongue deep into her mouth, then quickly got out of the car.

"Damn you," she giggled, "I'm going to make you pay for that."

I'm already paying. Lana had left me totally turned on. Standing in the street watching her drive away, I felt a sudden wave of depression come over me. What seemed to be a fantastic homecoming had quickly turned into a big letdown.

As I walked toward my parents' house, I couldn't get Lana out of my mind. Just thinking about her and remembering what I had just missed disturbed me greatly. After the way we parted, leaving me with blue balls, I just knew she would call in a few days. Those memories of her hand and lips were enough to re-stimulate me. But, until she called, I was going to need a quick fix.

Finding the key to my parents' cottage was where they always left it. I let myself inside. Still highly stimulated, I tried to make myself comfortable by having a beer. Grabbing one from the fridge, I went into the living room and turned on the TV. After turning on the television, I lay on the couch and sipped my beer.

It wasn't long before I heard my parents' car pull into its parking spot. Wanting to surprise them, I met them at the door as they entered.

"Bruce!" Mom cried.

Throwing her arms around my neck, my mother smothered me with kisses. Dad just stood behind her, waiting for his turn. As soon as my mother released me, my father grabbed my extended hand. Ignoring my hand, he threw his arms around me.

"Welcome home, son," he exclaimed.

When my dad released me, I pulled him close for another bear hug.

"I love you guys," I told them.

"We love you too," they said in unison.

"What's for dinner?" I asked quickly.

Mom laughed.

"Same old Bruce," Dad said.

"Hey, it's been a while since I had a good home-cooked meal," I uttered.

"Didn't your girlfriend cook?" Dad asked.

"Yeah, but it isn't mom's cooking."

"You sure know how to butter up your mother," Dad chuckled.

"That is what sons do, John," Mom said.

"While your mom cooks dinner, let's watch the rest of the game," Dad mentioned.

"Okay, John," Mom wined, with her hands on her hips, "Don't you change now that Bruce is home. That table needs setting."

Grumbling, but with a smile and a chuckle, Dad did what Mom wanted. When dinner was ready, we all took our seats, then, holding hands, Dad gave grace.

Once dinner was over, to be fair, I cleared the table as Dad did the washing. Finished clearing up, I helped by drying and putting the dishes away. While dad and I toiled in the kitchen, mom grabbed her favorite book, then curled up in her favorite chair to read.

Working in the kitchen didn't relieve my horny feelings. Lana had stirred inside me, and I couldn't let go. Those feelings, plus being without for so long, were enough to make me want to visit my old haunts, where I had hopes of finding some real enjoyment. If I couldn't find any enjoyment I was looking for, I would have to resign to going without until tomorrow.

Borrowing my dad's car, I left the house with hopes of getting lucky. Being gone for so long, I had no idea where to find an available woman. My first stop was at the tavern on the main drag. As I dove, I tried to remember back a few years.

Being a summer month, I knew all the bars in the area would be jumping, but I also knew most of the girls I knew would be taken, or gone.

Just as I was pulling into the parking area, my memory clicked. Some of his old friends told him of a place that they thought would be the best place for finding women.

Taking a chance, they were right, I got back on the main drag. As I drove, I hoped my old friends were right. Arriving at one of the places they told me about, I had trouble finding a place to park.

The bar had to be crowded. Loud shouts and laughter could be heard over the louder music. Finding one small spot, I squeezed into the only parking space I could find. After locking the car, I made my way

toward the entrance.   The closer I got to the front door, the noise and
the loud music got louder.

EIGHT

BRUCE

Entering the establishment, I found, not only were the lights very dim, but the smell of old booze and cigarettes filled the air. Standing off to one side, I let my eyes adjust to the din. Looking around, now that my eyes were adjusted, I began in earnest to search for possibilities.

The dance floor was crowded, and the bar stools were full. With shouts and laughter filling the air, a few seats became vacated. The space was a small space, but I did manage to squeeze up to the bar. Booze was flowing freely. Half the people in the establishment were already drunk or at least well on their way.

I was bumped into several times by people who couldn't walk straight. Most of the bodies bumped into me, ignored the situation, and kept moving. Deciding to move, as I stepped away from the bar, a sudden jolt occurred.

Out of nowhere, a girl came flying across the room in front of me. Acting as if she were shoved, she staggered helplessly in front of me. If she hadn't collided with me, I wouldn't have heard her scream. Instinct quickly took over. Grabbing her arm before she crashed into the tables, I did my best to steady her.

"Whoa there," I said.

"Ooh, thank you," the girl sobbed.

Now that she was steady on her feet, she did her best to smile, even though her eyes were full of tears. The girl was very pretty, but tall and skinny as a rail. Curly brown hair surrounded her pretty face.

"Take your hands off her. She is mine," some guy said, pushing his way to her.

"Whoa there," I said obstinately, "I think that is for the girl to say, don't you?"

"She is with me," the guy snarled again.

Ignoring the guy, while holding my own, I looked at the girl.

"My name is Bruce," I told her, "Do you want me to leave you alone?"

"No," she sobbed.

Facing the guy, the girl took a deep breath to control herself, then, before saying something, she stepped closer to me.

"This is the last time I'm letting you abuse me, Derrick."

"You are making a mistake, Gail."

Instantly, I knew the guy was a complete jerk. Hating jerks and their abusive ways, I blocked the guy's movement as he tried to forcefully grab the girl's arm. Instinctively grabbing the coward's arm, I stopped him.

"If I were you, I would let the woman go," I told him forcefully.

Trying to ignore me, the coward faced the girl. Veins were popping in his neck.

"If you go with him, we are done," the coward said, as he released the girl.

Stepping between them, I faced the coward. Threatening the jerk wouldn't do any good, but I did anyway.

"After tonight, if I find you have done anything to this girl, I'll hunt you down and make you sorry," I told him.

The jerk's face quickly turned to fear. He looked for help from his friends at the bar. At that moment, the girl's hand grabbed my arm from behind. Placing my hand on hers, I kept my eyes trained on the jerk.

He was looking and acting like the coward I knew he was. I also knew, if I turned my back, the coward would take a swing at me. Cowards never hit a man facing them. A coward will always wait until the other guy isn't looking or his friends come to his aid.

"Get lost," I growled.

The coward couldn't move quick enough. Because my training took over, I never took my eyes from the coward. Watching the coward slink away, he went to the bar where his so-called friends were. Still, I didn't see any movement.

The coward joined a few other punks at the bar. Gathering them close, they began to talk. At that moment, I thought I would have to be ready for anything. As it turned out, none of the cowards had the guts to make a move.

In my book, all of them were cowards. All the group could do was stare at me. Still feeling the girl's hand, still clinging to my arm, I turned to face her.   Looking into the girl's eyes, I saw nothing but absolute terror written all over her face.

"Do you want to leave?"

"Yes," she cried.

Taking her hand, I quickly led her to the door. Once outside, where we didn't have to worry, I looked into her eyes. The only thing I could see was terror. All of a sudden, she began crying. It was hard enough to give me concern.

NINE

BRUCE

"You are safe now," I told her.

Putting my arms around her, just to give her a little comfort, I waited for her to get under control.

"Please don't leave me here," she cried, "They know where I live and I'm scared they will come for me."

"Where would you like me to take you?"

"I don't care. Just don't leave me alone."

"How old are you, Gail?"

"I'm eighteen."

"You don't look a day over fourteen or fifteen."

"I just graduated from high school and turned eighteen three weeks ago."

"Doesn't that place card girls, who look so young?"

"Normally, yes, but not me. Derrick's father owns the bar."

"Is that so. I have a feeling his father is going to lose his business license."

"You had better be careful," she warned, "Taking me from Derrick was bad enough. You could be in for a lot of trouble."

"Trouble doesn't scare me," I told her.

"Please," Gail said in a panic, "Take me away from here, before they come looking for me."

"Where do you want to go?"

"Take me wherever you are going," she said.

"I can take you to my parents' house. They will be there and you should be safe, at least for tonight."

"Can we get a room somewhere?"

"That wouldn't be a good idea," I told her, "I'll take you to my parents' house."

"I don't want to go there," she sobbed.

"It would be the safest place for you," I told her.

"I want to stay with you," she sobbed.

"Gail," I said, holding her shoulders and staring into her eyes.

"I never sleep with a woman and not have sex with her."

"Having sex with you won't bother me," she said.

"You don't know me, Gail. I could be worse than those guys ever thought to be. I could be a murderer."

"But you're not."

"How do you know for sure?"

"The way you protected me tells me you aren't really a bad guy," she said.

"Damn. I can't leave you anywhere on your own, and I know sleeping with you will be a mistake. Do you have any other options?" Bruce asked.

"Please, let me stay with you tonight. Tomorrow, if you drive me to Hartford, I can stay with my grandparents."

"Why don't I take you there tonight?"

"It is too late. They will be asleep."

In a quandary, I drove out of town for two reasons. One was to give me time to think. The second, I was horny. In my thinking, I had to ask myself, why was I out tonight in the first place. What I wanted was already sitting in this car, in the seat next to me. All I would have to do is get a room. The girl sitting next to me was very pretty, maybe a little young, but she was legal and willing.

At that moment, I knew what I was going to do. A little further down the road, I saw a sign for a gas station. I was going to stop and hope they had what I needed. As I pulled in, Gail got a little scared.

"What are we stopping for?" Gail asked.

Quickly slinking down in the seat to stay hidden, I knew she was scared I would leave her.

"I need to get something," I told her.

Luck was with me. There on the wall was a condom vending machine. If I were going to have sex with Gail, I had to be sure I was protected. Even for another reason, if she is clean, I want to be sure I didn't get her pregnant.

I bought a pack, even though I didn't use them all. Getting back in the car, I drove another ten miles out of town, just to be on the safe side. In the distance, through the trees, I saw a sign for a motel. Pulling under the overhang, I stopped and got out. Not wanting to look suspicious, I walked casually into the office for a room.

There wasn't any problem. No questions, so I wrote my own factitious name. With the key in my hand, I drove to the room we would be sharing tonight.

"Here is the key," I told her, "Go inside and wait. I'm going to park out of sight."

TEN

BRUCE

As Gail slid out of the car, she had a look on her face that told me she didn't think I was coming back. She thought I was dumping her. Fear covered her pretty face, and she began to sob.

"I'm not going to ditch you, if that is what you are thinking," I told her, "I need to hide this car, so it won't be seen from the road. When I come back, I'll knock twice, then three times."

I waited and watched until Gail had entered the room. Then, driving behind the motel, where the car couldn't be seen, I parked and locked the car. Retracing my steps, I knocked twice, three times. It didn't take Gail to let me in.

"God, I am so glad you didn't leave me alone," she cried.

Happy, she threw her arms around my neck. I couldn't help but feel the hardness of her body. She had to be all skin and bone.

"Did you really think I would get a room, then leave you on your own?"

"I really didn't know," she sobbed, "Derrick would have."

"What kind of guys do you date?"

"Look at me," Gail said, "Would you date me?"

Spreading her arms, she twirled to give me a view of her body.

"Do I look desirable to you?" she asked.

"You're not hard to look at," I told her.

"Then why don't you want sex with me?"

"Being with guys like Derrick isn't a good reference for you," I told her.

"I don't have a disease, if that is what you are worried about."

"A guy can't be too safe."

"You don't have to fuck me, if you don't want to."

"I can't sleep in the same bed with you and not want sex."

"I'll sleep in the other bed."

"As you can see, there is only one bed."

"Oh yeah. It looks like we have to fuck, even if you don't want too," she said.

"I never said I didn't want to," I told her.

"Then what is the problem. Am I too skinny? Do you think I'm not built like other women?"

"Oh hell," I groaned, "Let's not argue."

Even with tears forming in her eyes, she began undressing.

"Hold it," I said suddenly.

"What's the matter? Are you changing your mind?"

"No, I'm actually looking forward to having sex tonight."

"So, what is the problem?"

"I'm hungry. Looking at you, you must be starving."

"Actually, I am starving."

"What kind of Pizza would you like?"

"I'll eat anything you order," she said.

Not wanting anyone to see them together, I phoned in a Pizza and beer. As we waited for the Pizza, we sat close together on the bed and turned on the television. Almost twenty went by before the Pizza arrived.

Meeting the pizza delivery guy at the door, I paid him. Going back to the bed, I sat. When it arrived, I ate a couple of pieces, leaving the rest for her. When she was full and we had our beers, Gail stood.

As if it were the natural thing to do, she began undressing. The more I saw of her, the better she looked. She was tall and skinny, but she did have some cute, little, feminine curves.

My desire for her quickly became very evident. Forgetting the Pizza for now, I undressed. Standing there stark naked, when her eyes saw what she was getting, they widened. When I dropped my shorts, it was quickly evident I didn't have any problem being ready.

"Man," she said, "I like what I see."

"I like what I see, too," I told her."

Once we were in bed together, Gail didn't just take it lying still. Foreplay was a must for her. It wasn't until I penetrated her, she went wild. Her movements were so wild, I had trouble establishing a rhythm. To my surprise, Gail climaxed three times before I could finish.

ELEVEN

GAIL

The day started off badly for me.   First off, Derrick was in a bad mood when he picked me up.   From the smell on his breath, I could tell Derrick had already been drinking.   When he drank so early, Derrick got nasty, and that was bad for me.

With nothing else to do and being afraid of Derrick, if I didn't go with him, I would have gone with him.   Arriving at the bar his father owned, Derrick didn't stop drinking.   A few of his so-called friends showed up at the bar, which meant he would be ignoring me, which was all right with me.

Normally, when Derrick and his friends meet, that mean trouble for me, or anyone else for that matter.   Derrick was known to start a fight and punch me out if I annoyed him, and that was always.   Worse yet, if he really wanted to hurt me, and he has many times before, he would use me as a sex object for his friends.

Knowing what Derrick was capable of, I tried to stay away from him when he was like that.   Being underage and not liking the taste of booze, I always drank soft drinks, that is, until Derrick forced me to drink something hard.

Once or twice, when some of his guy friends from out of town asked me to dance, I tried discouraging them.   When the guy is insistent, I would take the chance and dance with him.   Even Derrick's so-called friends, knowing what Derrick is like, would not dare ask me to dance.

One time, while I was dancing with one of his out-of-town guys, Derrick pulled me out of the guy's arms.   That only happened when the guy and I were on the floor.   It was like Derrick was looking for a fight. When the guy complained, Derrick broke his nose.

"Shut the fuck up," Derrick growled, "she's my girl.   If you don't like, get the fuck out of here."

Afraid and holding his nose, the guy would always leave the bar. After something like that happens, Derrick would always remain in his ugly mood.   Then he would be looking for someone to take his anger out on. I knew what was going to happen; Derrick always took his frustration out on me.

The last time that happened, for some reason, after Derrick slapped me, and I slapped him back without thinking much.   The shock of being struck by me only doubled his anger.   Doubling his fist, he hit me so hard I started to stumble back across the room.   As I stumbled backward, I happened to bump into someone.   That person, with quick reflexes, caught me before I crashed into the crowd.

"Whoa there," the guy said.

"Oh, thank you," I sobbed.

Even with a quick glance, I got a look at the man who grabbed me. He was very big and very handsome.   Once the man had me steady on my feet, I couldn't help but smile at him.   The guy was huge with a lot of muscle.

"She is mine, buddy," Derrick said, pushing through the crowd.

"Whoa there," the guy said obstinately, "I think that is for the girl to say, don't you?"

"She is with me," Derrick snarled again.

Derrick was used to getting what he wanted.   His fists were doubled, and the veins in his forehead looked as if they were ready to pop.   Even noticing the warning signs, the guy stayed there just daring Derrick to make the first move.   He never flinched.

Turning to me, the guy said, "I'm Bruce, do you want me to leave you alone?"

"No," I sobbed.

Turning back to Derrick, the guy moved between Derrick and me.

"It looks like you lost," Bruce said.

I was frightened for the guy. Yet relieved when the guy put himself between Derrick and me. What the guy was doing only made me stronger. Taking a deep breath, I got myself a little under control. Derrick tried stepping around the guy and was blocked. That was when I let Derrick know how unhappy I was.

"This is the last time I'm letting you abuse me, Derrick," I shouted at him.

"You are making a grave mistake, Gail."

Then Derrick grabbed my arm. Quickly, Bruce grabbed Derrick's arm to stop him.

"If I were you, I would let the woman go," Bruce said forcefully.

TWELVE

GAIL

Derrick was again facing the guy, almost nose to nose. The veins, popping out of Derrick's neck. Derrick's forehead looked like it was ready to explode.

"If you go with him," Derrick told me, "We are done."

With Bruce between Derrick and me, Derrick slowly back away. It would be the first time I ever saw Derrick back away from a fight. He probably knew he wouldn't win.

"After tonight," Bruce threatened, "if I find you have done anything to this girl, I'll hunt you down and make you sorry."

To make sure Derrick knew where I stood, I grabbed Bruce's arm. Then, to let me know he was backing me, Bruce immediately placed his hand over mine.

"Get lost," Bruce growled.

As impressed with Bruce as I was, I was still afraid of what could happen. Yet, Bruce never took his eyes off of Derrick, not for a moment. Then, Derrick sheepishly slithered off toward the bar. Only when Derrick had moved within to his group of buddies did Derrick glance back at the two of us.

Even then, Derrick's group of four never made a move toward us. It wasn't until Derrick and his friends turned their backs on Bruce that

Bruce turned to face me.   What Bruce saw, written all over my face, must have changed his mind.

"Let's get out of this place," Bruce said.

Taking my hand, he led me to the main door.   Once outside, as we moved to his car, I broke down and cried.

"You are safe now," he told me.

"Please don't leave me," I cried, "Derrick knows where I live and I'm scared he will come get me."

"Where would you like me to take you?"

"I don't care.   Just don't leave me alone."

"How old are you, Gail?"

"I'm eighteen."

"You don't look a day over fourteen or fifteen."

"I just graduated from high school and turned eighteen three weeks ago."

"Don't they card girls, who look so young?"

"Normally, yes, but not me.   Derrick's father owns the bar."

"Is that so.   I have a feeling his father is going to lose his business license."

"You better be careful," I warned him, "Taking me from Derrick was bad enough.   You could be in for a lot of trouble."

"Trouble doesn't scare me," he said, "Get in."

Bruce offered for me to stay with his parents for the night. Afraid of being found there, I pressed Bruce a little harder to take me with him.

"Now that I told Derrick off, I think I need to get as far away as possible," I cried.

Those words made him think a little. Then he changed his mind and gave in to me. Without so much as another word, he began to drive out of town.

As he drove out of town, I began wondering where he was taking me. In a way, I trusted him. But all this still made me feel nervous. Bruce was hard to read. But then, I know Derrick, and I didn't trust him.

The further we got out of town, the more I thought, maybe he did want sex with me. That wasn't going to be a problem for me. As much sex as I have been forced to have, with so many of Derrick's friends, one more time with Bruce wouldn't be a problem.

Now that Bruce was driving so far out of town, I wasn't sure what he wanted. In the beginning, I knew he didn't want sex with me. Then he stopped at a gas station. He didn't get gas, so what was he after? Maybe he needed to stop to pee. Whatever he did, he didn't take too long.

When I came back, I decided to keep my mouth shut and let whatever happens, happen. Further on down the road, Bruce pulled into the motel. When he went inside the office, I didn't know what to think. I knew he was getting a room, that was for sure, but was he going to dump me or sleep with me?

Waiting in the car was hell. One part of me thought, he is going to dump me. But the other part of my thinking was, he was going to sleep with me. What would sex be like with an older man? As strong as he is, would he hurt me?

When Bruce came back with a key in his hand, all I could do was wait until he did whatever he was going to do. As he got back into the car, he never said a word; he just drove to the room he had just rented.

"Go into that room and wait, I'll be right back," he said, "I will knock twice and then twice again. That is the signal that it is safe to open the door.

Knowing what he said made me feel safe.   At this point in time, I didn't have a choice.   Getting out of the car, I just knew he was ditching me.   With nowhere else to go and happy to be away from Derrick, I entered the room anyway.   At least I would have a warm, dry place to rest and take a shower.

Frightened and wondering what I was going to do tomorrow, I sat on the bed.   Deep down, I was hoping Bruce didn't ditch me.   A couple of minutes later, two knocks, followed by two more knocks, told me he didn't ditch me.

Those knocks made me scramble from the bed.   As fast as I could move, I rushed to open the door.   Seeing him, I flung my arms around him and cried.   To my surprise, he hugged me back.   After that nice hug, he released me.

"Are you hungry?" he asked.

"Yes, I haven't eaten all day."

"It shows," he said.

"What kind do you like?"

Then, with his cell phone, Bruce ordered the Pizza and two beers. Twenty minutes later, there was a knock on the door.   Bruce had me disappear when he answered the door.   Taking the Pizza, he paid.   Only once the guy was gone, Bruce called me.   Starving, I ate just a couple of pieces.   Bruce only ate two pieces, and I finished the rest.

My heart began a wild beat, as I watched him undress. Seeing him

Naked, I couldn't believe my eyes.   Not only was he good-looking, but he had a huge dick.   In bed, he showed me what foreplay was.   When the time came and he moved over me.   I wasn't too sure he would fit.

My fears were dashed.   Bruce took his time.   Finally, he penetrated me. The feel of him sinking so deep inside me was enough to make me climax.   It was the first climax I ever had.

He took me in different positions. Each time was a first for me. I couldn't help but give him a great ride. I had four climaxes before he finished. Now I was wishing he had gone bareback. Having a child by him would have been perfect.

THIRTEEN

BRUCE

Coming out of a deep sleep, my memory wouldn't let me forget what happened last night. Because of what happened, I felt great. The sex was better than good. Now, lying next to her, I had to have her at least one more time before we left this room. Rolling to face her, I was surprised to see her awake. With a big smile, I put my arms around her.

"Good morning," I whispered.

"Good morning," she whispered back, "Last night was so good, I'm hoping you will want more this morning."

"I have to admit, you do know how to satisfy a man."

"You had me so hot. I couldn't help but be active," she said, "You are the first man I have ever had a climax with."

"Then I guess one more time is what we both need," I told her.

Still feeling somewhat tired from last night's enjoyment, I held her tightly as she rolled me to my back.

"It's my turn to be on top," she told me.

When she quickly moved over me and straddled my hips, she chuckled. The feel of her warm wetness against my erection was fantastic.

With a deep moan, Gail raised her hips, put me just inside the lips of her vagina, and dropped on me.   As I slid deep inside her warm, wet cavity, I knew I was lost.

As she impaled herself, I could see from the look on her face the enjoyment she was receiving.   When Gail was filled, she flung her head back and uttered a cry.   Knowing she was fully enjoying it made me happy.   No sooner had I filled her when she began pumping her hips on me.

This time, it was easy to fall into an easy rhythm with her.   Going slow and easy, it was obvious Gail not only loved sex, but she knew how to get the best out of the man she was with.

Multiple climaxes seemed to be natural for her.   After my release, she rolled from me.   Feeling her lying so close to my side, I could hear her breath coming rapidly.   As we lay next to each other, totally satisfied, I closed my eyes to bask in total pleasure.   Seconds later, my eyes shot wide open.   Realization hit me.   We had just had sex, and it was bareback, no protection.

Being it was too late to worry about my mistake, my body told me I wanted her again.   When I rolled to put my arm around her, she quickly responded.

"Oh yea," she cried, "I can't get enough of you either."

When I moved over her, she quickly spread her thighs.   As I settled between her thighs, she wrapped her arms and legs around me, holding me in place.

"You do know we had sex without protection," I said.

She nodded a smile.   That smile told me she knew exactly what she was doing and wanted.   Knowing it was too late to worry about the mistakes now, I kissed her, then penetrated her again.

Again, we worked in a slow and easy pace.   She climaxed two more times before I gave her what she was crying for.   After a short rest, I felt her get out of bed.   Seconds later, I joined her in the shower.

Once dressed, I knew she had to be hungry.   After that workout, I knew she had to be famished.   Taking her to the small cafe, not far from the motel, I knew she felt extremely happy.   The look on her face and the soft melody she was humming told me she was feeling much better than she had last night.

Acting a little giddy, Gail moved in a young, lively step.   Her arm was through mine.   The smile she carried couldn't have been erased for any reason.

Waiting for breakfast, Gail couldn't erase the smile from her face. She even talked in a melodious voice.   It was a voice I had never heard before.   This girl was going to make some lucky guy a fantastic wife. While we ate, I could feel her eyes watching me.

"A girl could get used to a guy like you," she said.

"Gail, you are a much better person that you give yourself credit for. Find some guy who deserves you.   If you find the right guy, he will make you happy beyond what you feel right now."

"If we had more time together," Gail said, "I think I could make you as happy as you have made me."

"If I were looking for a woman to spend a life with, you would more than probably fit the mold."

"Then, I take it this is it for us," she said sadly.

I became worried about Gail, since she became unearthly quiet on the Drive.   The only time she said anything was when I asked for directions.

Two hours later, I dropped Gail off where her grandparents' home in Hartford.   We had to wait a few minutes after Gail rang the doorbell. An elderly woman with gray hair and a pretty smile came to the door.

"Gail!" The woman cried, "It has been so long.   It is so nice to see you again."

"It's nice to see you again, Granny."

Her grandmother immediately gave her a granny hug, then turned to me.

"And who might this be?" her grandmother asked.

"He is the guy who saved my life," Gail told her.

"Saved your life? What happened?"

"I was dating this guy, who I thought loved me," she sobbed, "He abused me now and then.   Then last night, this man put that jerk in his place."

"Don't you know this man's name?" her grandmother asked.

"Of course, I do, Grandma, he is Bruce."

"Just Bruce?   No last name?"

"My last name is Benson, ma'am."

"Then it is nice to meet you, Bruce Benson."

"Will you be safe here?" Bruce asked Gail.

"Yes.   Derrick doesn't know this place exists. Besides, my last name is different from Granny's."

"Good, then I should be on my way," I said.

"Will I see you again?" Gail asked.

"I doubt it," I told her, "I'm still in the military and I'm due to ship out any time now."

"Then, thank you for letting me be in your life, even if it was a short time.   You are a nice guy, and I promise to better my views of men."

"You are a good person, Gail.   Stay out of trouble and date some guy who deserves you.   Be happy."

I gave her another hug, then stepped back to close the door. With the door closed, I couldn't help but wonder what was going to happen to her.

FOURTEEN

BRUCE

On the ride back to town, my thoughts returned to Lana. Last night, while I was with Gail, a cute girl I enjoyed so much, I actually stopped thinking of Lana.   Now, alone again, Lana came back to mind.   Lana is a woman hard to forget, yet Gail had managed that in a few short hours.

If Lana wasn't so much older than me and already married, I could easily get interested in her. As much as I got to know Lana, in the short time we have spent together, I knew she wasn't in a happy marriage. The question was, would Lana ever be happy with just one man?

The drive took me nearly two hours to get to my parents' place.

By the time I got back, which was very late, I felt filthy and exhausted. Thank God, when I walked in, they were watching television.   When they didn't say anything, I went straight to my room.   Needing a hot shower and a change of clothes, I took advantage of the time.

After my shower and a change of clothes, I felt like a human again. Needing to spend some time with my parents, I joined them in the living room.   Because my mother hadn't spoken to me, it was evident that she was angry.

Dad greeted me with a smile, but not my mother.   Leaving her to herself, I figured, maybe she would be in a better mood in the morning, and went to bed.

For the first time in a long time, I didn't make breakfast. By the time I got up the next morning, my parents had already left for work. I did find something in the refrigerator to eat. After I ate, I went outside, looking for something to do. Seeing the shed, I started rummaging through it. A bike I had long forgotten about was hanging from the back rafters, where I had put it years ago.

Taking the bike down, I began to check it out. Everything seemed to be in good working condition, so I pulled it out. Then, going into the house, I changed into my swimsuit.

With nothing better to do, I threw a towel around my neck, then hopped on my bike. It had been a long time since I rode this bike, so the several miles I rode to the lonely beach were a killer. In my mind, I could still see the beach as it used to be.

Arriving at the beach, I parked my bike in the bike stand. Getting off the bike, I could feel the tension in my legs. I hadn't had a workout like this in a long time. Gazing around for a moment, I was surprised to find it just as I remembered it. For a small beach, it was still clean and peaceful, not overly crowded.

About thirty yards from shore, the old raft was still floating, as it was when I was younger. Like it was back then, a handful of teens were on it playing 'King of the Hill.' That game, on a slippery deck, as I knew from experience, was extremely dangerous.

Needing to cool down, I ignored the teens and swam to the raft.

Climbing aboard, the teens tried ignoring me. Not saying a word, I perched myself on the edge of the raft. Letting my feet dangle in the water, I soon became relaxed.

It soon became obvious, I wasn't going anywhere. The teens soon gave up their game. A few of the players quickly swam back to the beach, while the remaining few stopped horsing around.

After a full day at the beach, I was feeling much better. A few hours later, I swam to shore. Picking up my towel, I sat in the sand to dry off.

After that invigorating ride here, I had to mentally get ready for the ride home.

As I stood, I could feel the ache from the journey here. Now I had a ride home. Without stopping, I climbed on my bike for the ride home. I hadn't gone very far when I felt the muscles in my legs start to protest.

I was never so happy to get back home. I was in the mood for a hot tub, but since we didn't have one, I had to settle for a hot shower. Once I changed into dry casual clothes, I felt like a new man with sore muscles.

Being the time was close to my parents arriving home, I went into the backyard to heat up the barbecue. While waiting for the coals to heat, I set the picnic table and put a cooler with sorted drinks by the table.

With everything set up, I went back into the cottage to prepare the burgers for dinner. It wasn't long before I heard my parents' car pull into their parking space. As a surprise, I rushed to the backyard to begin cooking the burgers.

"What is this?" my Dad said as he came into the backyard.

"I thought the two of you would enjoy a burger and a drink of your choice," I said.

"Oh goodness," Mom squealed, "It just happens, I made a potato salad."

"You sit," I told her, "I will get it."

"What is the occasion?" Dad asked.

"Nothing special, Dad. I just wanted to do something nice for the two of you."

"I take it you had fun last night," Dad teased.

"John!" Mom cried.

"Marsha, Marsha, Marsha, when are you going to learn?"

"You will embarrass him," Mom said, blushing.

"Dad won't embarrass me, Mom," I chuckled, "I get this all the time from the guys at the base."

"Men," mom huffed, "I will never understand men."

"Men don't understand women either," Dad uttered.

Shaking her head, Mom went back into the cottage. Dad just laughed. It wasn't long before Mom was back to join us. Seeing Mom was back, Dad took one bite of the burger, then looked at it.

"God, what did you put in this meat?" Dad said, "It is utterly delicious."

"All I do is use a lot of garlic and black pepper, then cook it slow to keep it moist."

"I agree, where did you learn this?" Mom asked.

"From the girl I was living with," I said.

"What happened between you two anyway?" Dad asked.

"We grew apart," I told them.

"I guess I will have to use more garlic from now on," Mom said. "Is there any other tricks you have learned?"

"No."

"Is there anyone on the horizon? "Dad asked.

"There is one woman I could get interested in. But she is a lot older than me and already married."

"Have you dated this woman?" my mom asked perturbed.

"No. We had lunch once, but that is the extent of our relationship."

"Now that you know she is married, are you still going to date her?" Mom asked.

"Sure, why not. She isn't happy, and her husband has a girlfriend."

"How do you know this?" Mom asked.

"She told me."

"Bruce, we didn't raise you like that," Mom said.

"Marsha. Let it go," Dad said, "Men do what they do."

"Would you have done that, John?"

"Before we were married, I did."

"John! How could you?"

"The woman was absolutely beautiful, and I couldn't control my urges," Dad chuckled.

"What would you do now, if you got the chance to be with her again?" Mom asked.

"Nothing. I have the woman I want. I don't have those feelings for other women any longer, except for you."

"Mom, dad, cool it," I said, "Don't worry, I'm not going to do anything that would jeopardize her marriage."

"You will if you get caught," Mom said, "You might even get shot."

"I'm not about to put myself in a position where I will get caught."

"No one ever thinks they will get caught," Mom said.

"Mom, nothing has happened between us and probably never will. She is just a woman who captures my desires. You can't tell me you never had designs before you met and married Dad."

"That was different, the men weren't married," she said.

"Enough, Marsha, he is going to do what he wants, no matter what you think or want."

With a growl, my mom ate her food. She didn't have too much to say for a while, but I could tell she was angry. Letting her stew was the best answer. She probably will not forget, but she loves me. I know she will come around.

After the food was consumed, I began clearing the mess I had made, when my dad cornered me.

"I know you say what you feel, but next time, please don't talk about things like that in front of your mother."

"You got it, Dad."

"Is she really nice?" he suddenly asked,

"She is extremely nice and extremely beautiful. If she were single or divorced, I would definitely go for her."

"Well, don't get in any trouble," Dad said.

FIFTEEN

BRUCE

Knowing I would be upsetting my mother further if I went out again tonight, I decided to stay home and play table games with them. Staying home seemed to make my mother settle down a little. Once my parents had gone to bed, I knew my mother was still a little upset with me, but not as badly as if I had gone out again.

I went to bed feeling pretty good, but for some reason I had trouble falling sleeping. Even as early as I got up the next morning, Mom was up already making breakfast.

Sneaking up behind her, I gave her a hug.

"Oh, you men," Mom laughed.

"Did I scare you?" I asked as I grabbed a cup of coffee.

"Yes." She said.

Taking my seat at the table, I waited for my food. Since Dad was still sleeping, Mom and I started eating. As always, before we could finish, Dad finally crawled from his bed. Because my mother stopped eating to make dad something, I finished what I had. For some reason, my dad remained silent. Knowing my father, I knew my dad didn't want to stir the pot, so he kept his mouth shut.

"This Friday," my father said, "Do you have any plans for this weekend?"

"Not yet," I said.

After saying, not yet, I knew I had made a mistake. Just no, would have been the easiest answer. The look on my mother's face, when she came back into the kitchen, told me she had heard what was said.

"Will you be here when we get home tonight?" Mom asked.

Hearing my mom's question, my father left the cabin to go to the car.

"Most likely," I told her, "But if by chance I'm not, I will be sure to leave a note."

Before my mother walked away to join my dad, she just gave a I give up shake of her head, but she did hug me.

"I do love you, Bruce."

"I love you, too, Mom."

Not knowing how my father actually felt about my dating an older woman, I let it go. But it didn't seem to bother him as much as it bothered my mother. Now that my parents had gone to work, I had nothing to do but go to the beach. Dressed and ready to go, just as I was grasping the doorknob, my cellphone rang.

"Hello."

"Hi, it's Lana."

"Well, good morning to you, Lana," I said cheerfully, "I was beginning to think I would never hear from you again."

"Why wouldn't you hear from me?" she said, "You know how I was feeling about you."

"That was then. Today is another day, another time," I told her, "With your beauty, finding a man shouldn't be a problem."

"Are you saying you don't want to see me?" she asked.

"No way am I saying that," I answered quickly, "Not wanting to be with you, would never happen in this lifetime."

"Are you free today?" she asked.

"For you, I'll always be free," I told her.

"Great," she said happily, "Since you seem to know what I want, could you meet me at the Shamrock cabins?"

"Sure."

"I'll be in room ten," she said, "Just knock once and walk in. I'll be waiting with open arms."

Excited, I quickly climbed on my bike. Peddling as fast as I could, I made it to the Shamrock in about fifteen minutes. Pulling up in front of the room, she said she would be in. I rapped once, then entered.

What I saw the moment I opened the door stopped me cold. Lana was lying on the bed, facing the door, completely naked. The sight of her beautiful body sent my pulse racing. I couldn't believe what I was seeing.

For an older woman, with two children, a woman with still a fantastic shape. Seeing her as she was at that moment, let me see what her husband was missing and giving up. I didn't feel the least bit sorry for her husband. It was my win. In my mind, her husband obviously wasn't able to keep her happy. In my book, any man who didn't keep his woman happy didn't deserve her.

Sixteen

BRUCE

Quickly closing the door, I head straight for the bed. As I was told, I was being greeted with open arms and a beautiful smile. Not bothering to undress, I laid on the bed fully clothed. Lying with this naked beauty was making me extremely anxious.

After a quick kiss and hug, I quickly slid from the bed. I wanted to be as naked as she was. Quickly discarding my clothes, I was ready to return to bed. Leaving my clothes in a jumbled mess, where they fell, I stood naked before her for just a moment.

"My God," Lana groaned, "That is what I call a love muscle."

Joining her on the bed, she immediately rolled to her back. Opening her legs for me, I got a view that made me extra hard. The sight of her in that position made my mouth go dry.

Obviously, Lana was in no mood for foreplay. Beckoning me with open arms, I didn't want to waste time either. Now, I was hoping there would be a second time. I want to love every inch of her. Her actions told me everything I needed to know.

On the bed, I quickly took her into my arms. The feel of her warm, naked body against mine made me want to hurry. As much as I wanted and needed her, at this moment, I had a difficult time holding back my lust.

As our lips touched, I found her lips as warm and moist as any lips I had ever kissed. The feel of her short, compact body pressing against mine almost put me in orbit. My hunger for her was to hurry, and I found it very difficult to control. Even though my need to take her was so powerful, I knew rushing her wasn't the way to go.

Instead, I did my best to tease her. I wanted her beyond any resistance. She will have to beg for it, even if it meant torturing myself too. I knew there wouldn't be any resistance.

"Oh God, don't make me wait so long," Lana moaned, "I've been waiting for you since the day I picked you up."

With my excitement raining so hard, I was finding it difficult to hold off. What I wanted at this time was to enjoy every curve. To keep Lana from ranting, I pressed my lips to hers, as my hands did the playing.

Taking my kiss with a heated passion, Lana quickly became the aggressor. Knowing I wanted her begging, I let my hands do the talking. In her need, she drove her tongue deep into my mouth. I had all I could do not to take her then.

Her breasts were small, but very soft and succulent. With a cry, Lana wrapped her arms and legs tightly around me. Pressure of her clinging and pressing her small breasts tightly against my chest had me going. My arousal was very evident; this heavy passion hit us like a firestorm.

Sliding my hands beneath her, I captured the soft, round cheeks of her bottom in my hands and squeezed. Lifting her hips from the bed, Lana had kept one arm around my neck and both legs around my waist.

Giving out a growl, like a wounded animal, her free hand worked its way between us. She wasn't to be denied. Her free hand found what it was looking for. Grasping me tightly, she quickly placed me into position.

"Damn you, Bruce, do it now," she groaned.

Her position made it easy for me to make the connection. With one thrust, I sank deep inside her.

"Oh my God," she cried.

To my amazement, she felt very tight.   Her warm wetness allowed me easy entrance.   No sooner had I completed my penetration than she began driving hips.   The feeling was sensational.

Deep and tightly pressed together, we didn't have to thrust so hard against one another to find our pleasure.   Just the feel of her enveloping me was enough.

"Give it to me hard," she cried.

After what seemed like only seconds, from the time I filled her, she began to shudder.   A sudden scream, from deep inside her, rented the air.

"Lord be with me, I've died and went to heaven."

In climax, Lana's body bucked harder beneath mine, while her head rolled wildly on the pillow.   Wanting more out of her, I quickly placed her legs over my shoulders.   Now she was in a position to take me as deep as I could go.

"Jesus H, I never knew. I never knew," she kept crying.

I was in as far as I could get.   My thrusts became harder and deeper. Lana quickly screamed a second and third time.   Not finished with her yet, I pulled from her.

"Jesus, come back in," she cried.

Immediately, her eyes begged him to come back inside her. My need to climax was so close, I was afraid to continue my onslaught.   Rolling to my back, I pulled her with me.   Her eyes were now glazed over with passion. Not wasting any time, she straddled me. She didn't hover over me, moving her hips in a way that drove me wild.   With no wasted motion, Lana took me deep, as deep as she could get.   Immediately closing her eyes, her head rolled back, as she bellowed out in complete ecstasy. The way she rolled her hips on me, my erection quickly began to swell.   It was evident I was about to climax.

"Ooooh Gooood damn," she screamed.

"I can't hold off Lana."

"Good, give it all to me," she screamed.

By sitting straight up on me, Lana pressed her body down on me. She took everything he had to give. Almost immediately, she screamed her own climax mixed with mine. It was at that same moment, I erupted deep inside her. Completely satisfied, instead of rolling from me, she collapsed upon me, putting her entire weight on my body.

Slowly, as their breathing came back to normal, Lana gave off with a deep sigh, then rolled away from me.

"Good God," she moaned, "I didn't know sex could feel so fantastic."

With those words, Lana rolled against me. Throwing a leg over my body, she clung tightly to me, and she began to cry.

"Why are you crying?" I asked.

"I am crying with complete happiness," she sighed, "This is the first time in my life, I have ever felt complete satisfaction. Why couldn't I have met you years ago?"

"If he had met years ago, I would have been too young for you," he told her.

"I hope this isn't the only time we can be together," she moaned.

Wrapping her tightly in my arms, I whispered, "I'll be available to you anytime you need me."

"Good," she cried.

"I still have two more weeks at home," I told her.

"I'm going to take as much advantage of that time as I can," she stated.

"Well, you have my number. All you have to do is call."

"You can be sure I will be calling you," she said, kissing me, "I am going to miss you terribly when you're gone."

"If you were single, I would take you with me."

"You're not driving back, are you?" she asked.

"No, but if you were going with me, I'd leave next week and make the trip a fun trip," I told her.

SEVENTEEN

BRUCE

ecause she had thrown her leg over me, her close contact was enough to quickly put me back in the mood. From the way we were lying together, I knew she could feel my erection returning.

"Do you want to shower together?" she asked.

"Shower?"

"Well, after the second time, we should shower," she giggled, "or we can do it in the shower."

Saturday morning came too quickly. Five times in one day completely drained us.

"Damn," Lana moaned, "I didn't know I could handle any man, five times in one day."

"You didn't seem to have any trouble," I told her.

I watched her slide from the bed. With a groan, she waddled to the bathroom.

"Damn," she moaned.

"Are you needing some rest?" I chuckled.

"Yes," she answered, "but... but if you insisted, I would help you out no matter how much it hurt."

Chuckling, I said, "Actually, you win.   I'm so drained, I couldn't go again right now anyway.   Maybe I could later tonight."

Of course, the night together never happened.   Lana had to get home. As for me, I had to spend some more precious time with my parents before I left. Since meeting Lana, she has left an impression on me that I have never felt with any woman I have slept with.

Sadly, I knew I was actually too young for her, or she was too old for me.   Either way, I would always have these memories of Lana.

Now that our time was up, I had to let her go. I didn't want to, but I had to.

Watching Lana drive away made my head spin. How could any man, let alone her husband, be so God damn blind not to see what he has in her?   What is it she does that makes him unhappy, to look for another woman?   As far as I can see, she goes out of her way to make her man happy.

What would make any man turn to another woman when he had everything he needed at home?   Was it possible that her husband didn't know how to satisfy a good woman?   Lana has just given me some of the best sex I have ever had in the short time we were together.

Still early in the day, I needed a change of something to do. On the spur of the moment, I rode to the river. Renting a boat, with a trolling motor, I bought bait, then headed the boat to the mouth of the river, where I knew the fishing was good.

Even though the fishing is usually good at the mouth of the river, I really wasn't expecting to catch anything. My head wasn't in the game. I just needed to do some deep soul searching, something different, some time alone to think of where my life was taking me.

Going a few hundred yards from the mouth of the river to anchored on the sand flats, I threw in my line.   I sat back, waiting for a bite, pondering the way things were going.

It wasn't long before I got lucky.   Feeling a tug on the line broke my chain of thought.   Reeling in my first catch.   It was a three-pound flounder.

Two hours later, after a lot of thinking and three more fish, I had enough for dinner.   Hauling in the anchor, I rode back to the dock.

Knowing I wasn't going to see Lana anymore this weekend, my catch slung over the bars of my bike, I rode home.   Once home, I got the fish ready for cooking.   Making dinner for my parents was going to be easy. After rolling the fish in egg and covering them with cracker crumbs, I placed the fillets in the refrigerator to keep them cool.

Just as I was putting the fillets in the refrigerator, I saw my mom had already made her favorite potato salad.   Being the weather wasn't too hot or windy, I went out back and took the time to put the picnic table in the shade behind the house.   With everything ready to go, I still had two hours before they got home.

Feeling weary, I collapsed on the couch to watch a ballgame. Sometime later, I heard my name being called.   Then, I felt someone pushing me.   It was as if he were in another world.

"Bruce, Bruce, wake up."

Suddenly, as I began coming back to reality, my eyes snapped open.

"Wake up," the voice kept saying.

EIGHTEEN

BRUCE

Having been in one hell of a dream, I couldn't completely come out of the dream. Struggling to wake, it took a few moments to realize where I was. Then, gazing into my mother's eyes, I realized what was going on.

"Are you okay?" she asked.

"Oh, yeah," I said groggily.

Rolling to put my feet on the floor, I sat on the edge of the couch. From sleeping so hard, I felt dazed.

"Where is Dad?" I finally asked.

"He is cooking the fish you caught."

"Shoot. I'm sorry. I didn't mean to fall asleep," I mumbled.

"You must have needed the nap," Mom said.

Standing, I automatically hugged my mother, then hurried out the back door.

"Hey, Dad, I'll take over."

"Everything is ready," Dad told me, "That is why I had your mom wake you. Take a seat."

At that moment, Mom came from the house carrying her potato salad. The only thing missing were the drinks. Rushing back into the house, I grabbed three bottles from the fridge. Outside, I placed them on the table where my parents were already sitting.

"Thanks," Dad said.

Taking the bottle, my dad took a large sip, then wiped the sweat dripping from his face.

"I'm going to have iced tea tonight, Bruce," Mom said.

"Okay," he said, "I'll get it for you.".

"Sit, your food will get cold," she told me.

After dinner, since dad did all the cooking and mom, being mom, I cleared the table and began washing what little dishes there were to wash.

"Aren't you going out tonight?" Mom asked.

"No, I am going to spend this evening at home with you and Dad."

"What would you like to do?" she asked.

"I don't care. We can play games or watch television."

"Where is your new girlfriend?" Mom asked.

"Unavailable," I told her.

"Is she the married woman, or are you dating some single girl?"

"I'm not dating any girl, Mom. I just go out with any girl who wants to have fun."

"I won't ask you what your definition of fun is," Mom chuckled.

"Mom, are you saying, all I want is sex from a woman?"

"That is what it seems like. That is all you want."

"Mom, I do love sex, but if the girl I'm with doesn't want sex, then I don't get any. Sex is just added pleasure, that comes along when the woman is completely willing."

"Marsha, let it go," Dad shouted.

"I can see your son takes after you in that department," Mom said.

"You make it sound as if you don't like sex," Dad countered.

"I give up," she said.

Angry mom left the room. Moments later, she came back with her favorite book. Without a word, she climbed into her recliner, laid back, and began reading.

Turning on the television on low, so as not to disturb her, Dad and I turned our attention to the ballgame. It wasn't long before Mom fell asleep in her chair and began lightly snoring. Looking at Dad, I could see dad's head was beginning to nod.

"Christ, why don't the two of you go to bed?" I told them, "It looks as if you both need some sleep."

With a grunt, my parents disappeared into their bedroom. Now that the house was quiet, I quickly became bored with the game. Feeling tired myself, I decided it was time for me to get to bed too. Going to bed early was something I rarely did.

Just as sleep was taking over, a sudden loud crash brought me to a sitting position. Now, completely awake, I heard what sounded like a waterfall just outside my bedroom window. It was raining so hard that some of the spray was coming through the window. I hadn't heard a downpour so heavy in years.

Dashing from my bed, I quickly closed the window, but not before I was doused with water. Now wide awake, I went to the living room to check the rest of the house.

"Damn, the wind is strong," Dad said, coming from his room.

"This is definitely a quick storm," I uttered.

"It definitely did come quickly," Dad said.

We scrambled to be sure all the windows were closed. Then

, going out onto the front porch, we got a whiff of fresh, clean air. The sound of the rain pelting the pavement and roof, plus the smell of fresh rain, was relaxing. Standing at the railing, Dad and me, we watched the storm. Then, as quickly as the storm began, it disappeared.

Feeling a sudden chill, I went back to my room. Reopening my window, I slid beneath the warm covers. Listening to the light rain that was now falling and smelling the clean air, I found it easy to fall back to sleep.

Early the next morning, awakened by the smell of my mom's cooking, I glanced at the clock on the table next to the bed. It was a little past eight. Never had I slept so long. If it wasn't for my mother's cooking and the fact that rain was still falling, I would have preferred to burrow down beneath the covers for some extra sleep. But, smelling coffee and bacon, I was forced to climb from the bed.

"Good morning, Bruce," Mom said as I entered the kitchen.

"Good morning, Mom."

Coming up behind her, I wrapped my arms around her waist, and I hugged her tightly.

As I pulled her close, my mother, feeling my body behind her, let her head fall back against my chest and uttered a sigh.

"The food will get burnt," she chuckled.

"Am I really bothering you?"

"No. I really do miss your hugs and your strength, Bruce. Your dad doesn't do that much anymore."

"He doesn't know what he is missing," I teased.

Turning off the stove, Mom turned in my arms. Wrapping her arms around my neck, she pulled my head down to give me a sweet kiss.

"If you weren't my son," she teased.

"Mother!"

Laughing, she said, "Take your seat."

Mom swatted my butt as I turned from her. At that very moment, my dad came from the bedroom.

"I smell heaven," Dad uttered.

"Well, sit down and load up," Mom sang, "I can make more."

It turned out to be a quiet weekend. The three of us played cards for two days and munched on anything we could find. Early Sunday night, my parents went to bed early.

NINETEEN

BRUCE

It was still raining when I awoke on Monday morning. Mom and Dad had already left for work. Feeling warm and comfortable, I burrowed down for some added sleep. The way the rain was falling, I knew this was going to be a long, boring day.

To my sadness, it rained for three solid days. Since it was warm outside, on two of those days, just to break the monotony, I took a long walk in the rain, just wearing my bathing suit. Those who saw me must have thought I was crazy. When I returned, I didn't need to shower, so I changed into something warm and dry.

After lunch, I took another walk. It was Thursday, and the rain finally stopped. The storm did clean the air, but now the humidity soared, and mosquitoes came out in full force. Then the ringing of his phone startled me.

"Can you get away?" the voice said.

"Where are you?"

"On my way to you," Lana said, "I have the entire weekend starting today. Can you make it?"

"Where do you want me to meet you?"

"Meet me in front of the restaurant in half hour."

Hanging up, I quickly packed a small bag with underclothes. Wearing shorts, I put on a light top, then brought two other shirts just in case. Making sure I didn't forget anything, I wrote my parents a short note.

"Mom, I'm going out of town for a few days. This rain is making me feel stir crazy. I know I have only a short time left at home, but I need to get away. I'll see you in a few days. I love you both very much." Bruce.

Packed and ready to go, I made sure the cottage was locked and secure. Placing the note where I knew my mother would find it, I smiled, knowing the reaction the note would have. I felt sorry for my dad. Shaking my head, I went out the door, knowing my mom would undoubtedly fill in the unwritten words with her own thoughts. She would be right, but I wasn't about to tell her that.

Walking the short distance to the restaurant where I was to meet Lana, I only had a five-minute wait. As Lana pulled up, I saw that beautiful smile covering her face. Once she came to a stop, the trunk flew open. Without hesitation, I threw my bag inside, then quickly slid into the seat next to her.

Once I was seated, she unbuckled. Sliding over to me, she gave me a steamy kiss to let me know she missed me. Getting behind the wheel again, she growled. After driving a few miles out of town, she pulled over. Climbing from the car, she walked to the passenger side, where she opened the door.

"You're driving," she said.

No sooner had I climbed behind the wheel than Lana grasped me.

"I missed you terribly," she said.

As she began hugging and kissing again, she groped me. Her grope was so hard, she set my body on fire. Lana's attack left me feeling shattered, wanting and needing her badly. The warmth and softness of her body awakened my senses into a world I had never been in before. Those kisses, from her sweet lips, made me want to find the nearest motel. They were kisses I would never forget.

When she released me, I sat there in complete shock. When I came back to earth, I couldn't do anything but breath and that was difficult. Completely shaken, I couldn't think clearly.

"Are you shook?"

"Yes."

"After those kisses, I don't know really know if we will be able to make it to our first stop tonight," Lana said.

"Where is our first stop supposed to be?" I asked.

"The Cape."

"We have plenty of time to get there before it gets too dark," I said.

"That isn't what I was referring to," Lana chuckled.

"Would you like me to find a nice quiet place where we won't be disturbed?"

"I was thinking of something much more comfortable," she said.

"You have been on my mind all week," I told her, "I'll stop any time or place you tell me to."

TWENTY

BRUCE

Before I could drive away, Lana did it again. She quickly screwed up my concentration by sliding over closer to me. Ince there, she placed one arm around my shoulders and pressed a breast firmly against my arm. Then, intentionally, she pressed her warm thigh tightly against mine, while her free hand came to rest high on my thigh, touching my crotch.

"Okay, I get the idea," I exclaimed.

A few miles down the road, I pulled into the first motel I came to. Getting the room was easy. With a key in hand, we didn't waste any time getting into bed. It has been two long weeks since the last time. We went at each other, like wild animals.

Lana was overactive. She acted as if she couldn't get enough. Thrust by thrust, we quickly worked to our first climax. Moments later, Lana sat on the edge of the bed, leaving her body open to my view.

"I guess I had better call the motel and tell them we won't be there until tomorrow," Lana sighed.

I had just had more of the most satisfying sex ever. Sitting near her, totally naked, all we had to do was look at each other. We were unable to hold ourselves back. Just a touch was enough for us to be stimulated. With a moan, she came back to me.

"God, you make me into a wanton woman," Lana moaned.

"I know. I can't get enough of you either."

"Come to me, lover," she said, rolling back into bed.

My thoughts were, how could any woman, close to forty, be so beautiful, so alluring, and so lusty? Her husband had to be blind. Not wanting to separate, we spent the night making up for the two weeks we had been apart. Sometime during the night, exhaustion finally took over. Lying in each other's arms, we passed out.

We didn't awaken until past nine the next morning. After one more time, we were ready to go.

"Damn," Lana moaned, "After a night with you, I am finding it difficult to walk."

"Is that a complaint?"

"No, just a statement," she chuckled.

"We could rest for a day or two," I teased.

"Ha, ha, you are being funny," Lana said.

Kissing me, she said, "We don't have enough time together as it is. I don't want to miss one moment of this pleasure. Not for any reason."

After a quick shower, we made our way to the café. We held hands like two people on a honeymoon. Taking out time, we ate. With our energy replenished, we were on our way again.

Even after the lusty night, Lana glued herself to my side. I had a hard time concentrating on my driving, with her sitting so close. We stopped a couple of times to walk and explore. On our walks, we held hands or had our arms around each other.

"God, I'm going miss this," Lana cried, "I forgot what it is like, for fun-loving couples to have so much fun together."

On our first stop, Lana stopped by a small brook. Quickly pulling me to face her, she wrapped her arms around my neck, then pressed her soft, warm lips to mine.

"Get a room," a couple of kids hollered.

Laughter and clapping erupted from the crowd. Lana just looked at them and smiled. Then, looking at me, she said, "I think these people are jealous."

"I would be jealous too, if I was the other guy looking at the way you're are put together."

"Flattery is going to get you laid," she said, "when we finally get where we are going."

"It is going to get us both laid," I corrected her.

"Then, let's hurry. This talk makes me horny. Hell, just thinking of what is to come makes me horny," she moaned.

"And sore?"

"Yes, but the soreness comes from something worth getting sore for," she said.

"It's a good thing sex doesn't wear away a man's penis away," I chuckled.

"That is not funny. Think of all the fun people would be missing," she chuckled.

TWENTY-ONE

BRUCE

It was already Friday night by the time we finally made it to the Cape. Even as tired as we were, it didn't stop us from enjoying a beautiful night of love-making. Nothing is better than basking in the aftermath of something so beautiful. We laid locked in each other's arms, wanting to remain that way forever.

"We have just tonight and Saturday night," I whispered, "Then we will have to look for the long drive home."

"Damn," she moaned, "This weekend is going too quickly. I need more time alone with you."

"If we were married," I chuckled, "we would probably have a dozen kids already."

"With you pumping kids into me," she said, "I wouldn't care how many kids we had."

"Making kids is fun, but paying for them isn't," I stated.

"I know. I shouldn't say this, but my time for having kids is over. The two I already have, have been hard enough to raise, let alone having more at my age," she sighed, "I just hope, when you finally have kids, you have all boys."

"Because you said so, I will order nothing but boys."

She laughed.

"You make me feel so happy," she said, "I'm going to hate it when your gone."

"I'm going to miss you too, Lana," I told her.

Taking her into my arms, I pressed my lips to hers. It was a lengthy kiss.

"God, let's stop talking," she cried, "so we can enjoy what time we have together."

In the morning, when I opened my eyes, I was shocked to find Lana staring at the ceiling, crying. Taking her in my arms, I held her tightly.

"What's wrong, Lana? Are you feeling guilty?"

"I don't have any guilt for what I am so thoroughly enjoying. It is just that today is Saturday," she sighed, "Tomorrow we have to go home."

"I will still have a week before I have to go back," I told her.

"I want to spend the rest of your time home, with you," Lana cried, "and I can't. God, what have I gotten myself into? Falling in love with a man thirteen years younger scares the hell out of me."

"I'm falling in love with you, too, Lana," I told her.

"What are we going to do?"

"There isn't anything much we can do. You are still married, and I'm still in the military."

"When do you get out of the military?"

"My plans are to make a career of the military. The travel and benefits make the sacrifice worth it."

"How many years will that be?"

"I have at least seventeen years to go."

"That means you will be gone most of the time."

"Yes, but we can always make up for lost time when I get home," I told her.

"I'll have to think on this," Lana said, "I'm not getting younger. In seventeen years, I'll be fifty-one and you will be thirty-eight. Most of our lives would be wasted being apart. I can't see you living that long alone and not finding some younger girls to make you happy. Maybe the best for both of us to enjoy what we have now, then go our separate ways."

"Would it be possible for us to see each other when I do come home on leave?" I asked.

"I don't know. I guess that would depend on how often you came home," she said.

"I'll always love you and will never forget you, Lana."

"And I'll love and never forget you, too, Bruce. What you have given me, since we met, has been fantastic. I'll never forget what we had, but I need a man to be home with me every night."

"Your husband isn't home now."

"That is why I don't want another situation with those conditions."

"Then I guess this weekend will be the last of our last time together", I said sadly.

"Then let's enjoy what we have today," Lana said.

Satisfying their needs was first on the agenda. Knowing they would have to part after the weekend, they didn't stop being attentive to each other. Wherever they went, they held hands or had their arms around each other. Exhaustion from a day's trek didn't stop them from expending what energy they had left, making love.

Sunday morning, before breakfast, they were at each other again, with what they thought would be or last time. As before, I drove, but the trip home was quiet. Neither of us wanted this weekend to be over.

As she always did, when I drove, she would sit as close to me as she could get.

Every now and then, when I looked at her, tears were forming in her eyes. I was feeling as if I were about to lose everything. Being together like this was as if we were reliving our teenage years all over again.

The closer we got to home, the more I felt the sexual tension grow inside me.   Entering the last town, not far from where we were to part, Lana broke the silence.

"Bruce, pull into that motel," she said, "I need you, at least one more time, before we part."

"I'm glad, because my need for you is close to desperate," I told her.

Because neither of us wanted to part, we knew this stop would be our last time together.   Lost in our reasoning, we both cried and kissed, still unwilling to let the other go.

"I love you, Lana."

"And I love you, Bruce, more than you will ever know."

Fully sated, we left the motel with tears rolling down our cheeks.

At the car, Lana reluctantly took the keys to drive the last leg home. It was obvious our sadness was filling the air.   Leaving each other was going to be harder than either of us realized.   At the stop where I was to leave her, I turned in my seat to grab my bags. Sliding from the car, I felt as if my heart was being pulled from my body.

Outside, I walked around the car, only to bend over the door for one last kiss.

"Four days with you wasn't enough," I told her, "But it was the best weekend I ever had."

She was openly crying.   With a heavy heart, I knew this was going to be the last time we would see each other for a long time.   Weeping was something I couldn't control. After that last kiss, turning away from her was twice as difficult.

"I think you are forgetting something," she blubbered.

Unable to resist, I tried my best to smile.   Ricking my head in the window, I let our lips touch for the last time.   Our last kiss was sweet and tender. Our soft, wet lips lasted longer than normal. When I finally pulled away, Lana burst into tears.

As she drove away, I felt as if my heart was going with her.   Pulling out a hanky, I wiped my eyes.   It was the longest walk to the cottage that I ever took.

TWENTY-TWO

BRUCE

The moment I walked in the front door, I didn't have to look at my mother's face to know she was angry with me. Nevertheless, I gave her a hug to show her I love her, then quickly stepped back. I waited for her barrage.

"You had better change clothes," she said, "I can smell her on you."

Without a word, I went to my room to change. After taking a hot shower, I joined my parents in the living room.

"She must be one hell of a woman," Dad said.

"I don't want to hear about it," Mom said.

"We won't be seeing each other any longer," I told them.

"What happened?" Dad asked.

"She didn't like the idea of me staying in the military for seventeen more years."

"So, what are you going to do now?" Dad asked.

"All I can do is find another woman, one that will not only make me happy, but will understand and support my way of life."

"Do you think you will ever find a woman like that?" Mom asked in a nasty tone.

"There are a lot of women in this world, Mom. There has to be one woman out there that will want me for me, not what I do," I told her.

With nowhere to go or see, I spent my last week at home. During the day, I would go fishing, which we would have for dinner.

One day, I went to the beach to be alone and think. Staying busy didn't help. Lana was in his heart, and she would always be there. Finding loneliness was easy; it was driving me crazy. The question in my mind was, would Lana miss me as much as I am missing her?

The day of my flight, my parents took him to the airport. It was a very sad day for me and my parents. Mom tried not to let me see her cry while she wiped the tears from her eyes. Dad, who usually talks all the time, sat glumly behind the wheel. Me I'll miss them. In a way, I was sad I didn't spend as much time with them as I had hoped.

"I'll be home the next time when I receive my new orders," I told my parents.

Hugging my mother one last time, I said, "I love you, Mom."

Even though my mother was still angry with me, I knew she would eventually get over it. Releasing her, I could see the anguish in her eyes. Turning to my father, I could see my father's clench jaw.

"Have a good life, son," Dad said, "We will see you when you come home next time."

"You can count on that, Dad."

I didn't spend as much time with my parents as I wanted, because of meeting Lana. Most of my time was spent with Lana. Just the thinking of Lana was enough to give me a jolt to my system. The times I had spent with her were special. Thinking of just one special moment was enough to send erotic feelings surging through my groin. Forgetting Lana wasn't going to be easy, but I knew I had to.

On the flight back to my home base, I tried sleeping. I was awakened by the stewardess when we were getting ready to land. The moment I got off the plane, I noticed the difference in climate. The sky was clear, but the atmosphere wasn't as hot and humid as it was back home.

Walking through the crowded terminal, my only thought was, how in the hell was I going to get to Port Hueneme. Seeing a sign 'Greyhound', I made my way to the desk.

"Where do you want to go?" the girl asked.

"Port Hueneme," I told her.

"Oxnard is as close as I can get you," she said, "The bus station isn't far from the base."

Figuring the choice she had given me was good as any, I climbed aboard the bus. As the bus wound its way through the cities, it gave me an idea of how people on the West Coast lived compared to back on the East Coast.

Once the bus got to the freeway, I found the ride to Oxnard boring. There was hardly any greenery to be seen, mostly just barren landscape with scrub brush. Everything was brown. After seeing what I have seen so far, I began to wonder what the town I was headed to was like. Any town I got a glimpse of was in the distance.

When the bus pulled into Oxnard, I was amazed at the number of bars and motels there were. From the looks, I got off the bus in the middle of town. Apartment buildings and bars littered the streets on both sides. A few drunken Sailors roamed the streets with girls on their arms. Afraid to go anywhere until I got directions, I asked the girl behind the counter how he could get to the base.

"How do I get to the base?"

"Which base?" she asked.

"There are two bases?"

"Yes. There is Pt Magu and Port Hueneme."

"Port Hueneme," I told her.

"The easiest way to get there is by cab. The base isn't far."

Ten dollars got me a quick ride to the main gate. At the main gate, I had to report to the Petty Officer on duty. After reporting in and no ride available, I had to hoof it to the barracks. Miserable from the heat, I grunted as I threw my bag over my shoulder. By the time I walked into the barracks, I was exhausted and soaked with sweat. The walk showed me just how out of shape I was.

In the barracks, I dropped my bag. Handing the Master at Arms my orders.

"Where is your check-in sheet?" the master at arms asked.

"Where do I get that?"

"You have to go to the Personnel Office."

"Where in the hell is that?"

With a smirk, the Petty Officer glanced at the clock.

"You have an hour to get there before it closes. If you want, leave your baggage here. The Personnel Office is two blocks that way."

Already hot and miserable, I grumbled a bit before leaving the cool barracks. Knowing I didn't have a choice, if I wanted to get checked in, I sucked it up and left. Already soaked and sweaty and wanting to get this check-in out of the way, I jogged on tired legs to the Personnel Office.

By the time I got there, my uniform looked as if I had been swimming in it. Besides being dirty and sweaty, I was totally out of breath. Handing the second-class petty office on duty my orders, he looked at them, then handed them back.

"Your orders read MCB3," he said, "If you hurry, you can get to their office before they close. It is two blocks that way. You can't miss it."

"Thanks," I groaned.

Going out of the building, I was pissed. Couldn't anyone give me the correct directions? My uniform already sodden with sweat and feeling ten pounds heavier, I gave it all I had. Running out of time, I ran full tilt the two blocks to the office. Sweat was pouring from my brow, running into my eyes. My uniform looked like hell.

"Welcome aboard," the Chief chuckled, "What the hell did you do, run all the way?"

"Yes, after such a long walk, I didn't want to miss you," I gasped.

"Where are your bags?"

"At the barracks," I told him.

"Which barracks?"

"I don't know, the first one I came to."

"You're at the wrong barracks. Your barracks will be next door to where you left your bags."

"Damn," I grumbled.

The Chief laughed again.

"Relax, you have the whole weekend off. Report back to this building ready to go early Monday morning."

"Thank God," I moaned.

I had a long, miserable hike back to the barracks. Returning didn't seem as bad as going. Knowing I had the weekend off helped a little. When I finally got to the barracks again, I thanked the MA for holding my bags. Knowing this was my last move today, I trudged through the heat one last time.

The MA at my new barracks checked me in. Given a rack, I entered the dorm I was assigned to. Knowing not to leave stuff lying around, I filled my locker and my new foot locker, sitting in at the foot of the rack I was given. First things first, as tired as I was, I took a long, hot shower, then changed into something clean and dry.

No longer feeling like I had walked through hell and back, I was ready to crash, but I was starving. My hunger overrode my exhaustion. Leaving the barracks, I made my way to the chow hall, which was still open. Going through the line was disappointing.

The food wasn't bad. It was edible, but it just wasn't my mother's cooking. Nevertheless, I filled my belly. After appeasing my appetite, I now had an overwhelming thirst. At lunch, the milk, water, and coffee, and such weren't enough to quench my thirst. Sitting back, I tried to think of where to go to quench this thirst.

Then, remembering, as I was heading to the chow hall, I noticed a Bowling Alley not very far from the barracks. Leaving the Chow Hall, I walked the short distance to the Bowling Alley. At the Alley, I took the first seat at the snack bar. Ordering a beer, I turned in my seat to watch the bowling.

Chugging the first beer, I determined that, since everyone was wearing uniforms, it had to be league play. Finishing a second brew and feeling a hell of a lot better, I decided I had had enough. With my exhaustion catching up with me, I knew it was time to crash.

TWENTY-THREE

BRUCE

Feeling a little tipsy from the exhaustion and from the long day, after those two beers, it was time to hit the rack. Wearily, I made it back to the barracks. The moment my head hit the pillow, I was out.

Sometime during the night, sounds coming from other guys entering the barracks woke me. Being it was so late at night and there was no light on, I tried to get back to sleep. But hearing loud drunkenness, I was annoyed. Trying to ignore them, I put my pillow over my head. As tired as I was, I wanted to wait until morning to introduce myself.

Awake early the next morning, I could hear nothing but loud snores. Quickly getting dressed, I left the dorm. It was a brisk morning. Without something warm to wear, I walked briskly to the Chow Hall. Being early, there wasn't a long line. Walking leisurely to the serving tables, I took my time filling my tray.

Taking what I wanted, I sat alone to think about the things I needed to do over the weekend. With time on my hands, I decided to wait until later in the day, when it was warmer, to go to town. The one thing I was in the need for was a car. Since I didn't know the area, getting to town was going to be difficult. I would need someone to show me around town.

Leaving the Chow Hall, I had no idea where to go or what to do first. Again, hiking the base seemed the thing to do. Checking out the gym was a waste of time.   At this time of the day, no one was there.   The base seemed dead; nothing was happening.   Going back to the bowling alley was another mistake.   It didn't open until noon.

Knowing all this, hiking was futile, I told myself; at least I knew when everything opened and closed.   My last stop was the swimming pool. As I expected, the pool was closed until noon.   With nowhere else to go, I decided to hoof it to town, even if I did it alone.

After all the walking I did, the sun was high in the sky, and the heat was beginning to rise.   The bad part was, I had to walk.   Between the heat and being out of shape, I found the walk longer than I wanted.   Still, I knew the walking would do me some good.   It was better than spending money on a short taxi ride.

Walking out the gate, thoughts of Lana started to bombard me.   Why, all of a sudden, was her memory still haunting me?   Our relationship was supposedly over.   Realization quickly came to me.   To get Lana out of my mind, I was going to have to find someone to replace her, both physically and mentally.   To find that replacement, I would definitely need a vehicle.

Spending the entire day looking at vehicles at several different dealers, plus the walk getting to these dealers, was exhausting.   With limited funds, I quickly found I didn't have much of a choice on what I could afford.   To get the best for my money, I would have to spend almost all my savings.

After finding a reasonably good deal, I had spent most of my savings. Now, at least, I bought a car I really wanted.   Holding what cash I had left, I knew I still had to fill the tank.   After buying the car and filling its tank, I spent a couple of hours driving around, familiarizing myself with the town.

Still looking around, I drove to the pier in Hueneme.   Parking, I walked onto the pier.   Looking both ways from the pier, I found the beach seemed to stretch for miles, both ways.   Seeing several men, women, and children fishing from the pier, I decided to check out the fishing.

Finally, after a full day of excursions and a nearly an empty tank of gas, I drove to the place where I could get a sticker for my car. Finally, somewhat satisfied with my day, I drove back to the barracks. Finding a space to park, I locked up my prize.

Entering the barracks, I found it nearly empty. With nothing else to do and feeling sort of sleepy, I laid on my rack. Trying to get use to the time change was difficult, and I felt exhausted. Falling asleep as soon as my head hit the pillow, I slept through the night.

Monday morning, after a quick shower and shave, I had to get ready for muster. Being a third-class petty office, I was given a fire squad. As a fire team leader, I was in charge of three guys. It didn't take me long to learn some of the ropes.

With each man coming from different states, they each had separate personalities. Getting to know each man's separate personality wasn't easy. Some guys were easy to anger, while others were completely easy to be around. Then, there was always one guy in every group who loved to make trouble.

Once I figured out who that person was, I had to learn how to deal with that person, without alienating the other men. I quickly learned, the only way to deal with a troublemaker was not to give him as many breaks as the others. The good guys made life easier for me. Once I began working that system, most of the time, the troublemaker would change his ways.

Twenty-Four

BRUCE

At muster the next morning, a couple of weeks later, it was announced the battalion would be heading to Camp Pendleton for training in one week.   Being it would be my first training trip, I had no idea what to expect.

Life at Camp Pendleton turned out to be completely different from what I expected.   Everything we did gave us new challenges to learn. We had the rifle range, we had night shooting with tracers, we fired bazookas, and marched everywhere we went.   All in all, you learn a lot about the men in your fire team.

Each night, everyone had to stand at attention at the foot of their racks.   When the Sargent blew his whistle, everyone had ten seconds to get into their rack.   If anyone missed, the whole barracks had to practice for two hours.

Morning, everyone has to get out of their rack in ten seconds; if not, everyone has to practice two hours at night.   Needless to say, those who screw up morning or evening and make everyone pay for their tardiness, pay hell the next day.

After a few weeks, the battalion returned to its home base.   Now that training was completed, it was announced that the battalion would be deploying to Okinawa in two weeks.   Being single, deploying wasn't as difficult; for married guys, it was difficult.

This would be my first deployment.   In one way, I was looking forward to being in a foreign land, learning their customs and their language.   As always, there are a few guys who hate going to a place they know nothing about.   They are the trouble makers, and that makes it hard on the ones willing to learn.

Flying into Kadina air base, I found the air in Okinawa very sultry. Getting off the plane, we had to form for our first muster, to make sure everyone made it safely.   From there, we were transferred to waiting buses. We ended up at a base, not far from the air base, called Camp Kinser.   Again, we fell in for muster.

Getting the Battalion quickly settled in was a headache. I was given a berth with three other guys, whom I was familiar with, but didn't really know.   Once we were settled, we had to muster to make sure everyone was still in camp. Once muster was over, everyone was release to their barracks to get squared away.

Job leaders had to report to their company headquarters to learn what jobs they would be doing.   Ince they knew a muster was held. Names are called.   My first job with the battalion was in supply.   My fire team and I had to report to clean up a mess left by the departing battalion.

Each crew was issued a toolkit.   My team and I had to make sure each toolkit had good working tools.   Once all the crews had what they needed, we had to go through the remaining tool kits to repair and replace missing tools.

Once everything was issued, we had to begin repairing the mess the last Battalion left behind.   Tool by tool was replaced, where needed, and new tools were procured.   In the beginning, the job became a merry-go-round.   Most of the tools left behind were in sad shape.   With a truckload of tools to repair the job turned into a headache.

As quickly as saws were sharpened, old saws were back for repair. Not caring about the tools, since they weren't theirs to begin with, the tools were readily abused.   New tools and parts were ordered weekly. It took my crew close to two months to catch up.   Requests for repairs and new tools slowed down.   From that time on, all new or repaired tools were placed in tool kit boxes and stored for further use.

The days moved quickly except Sundays.   Getting up at five every morning to shower and shave was a must.   Anyone not shaving, or without a haircut, or with their uniforms needing pressing was given extra duty when everyone else had time off.

Muster was promptly at 0700.   Chow was served before muster.   If anyone missed chow, they had to wait until lunch.   Miss one meal, and the next time you will be sure to make chow.   Every day was a long day, from five every morning to five every evening, with two hours for lunch.

Most weekends were spent playing ball.   On a few occasions, unless the person had a duty, they were allowed to go to town for Okinawan food.   Many of the guys made the trip every day after work.   Most of those who went to town every night usually came back drunk.

The town was packed with bars and restaurants up down both sides of the street.   The bars are packed with girls, waiting on tables, serving drinks, and are available to dance, provided the guy buys them drinks.

Finding a girl for sex was easy.   As long as the guy bought the girl drinks, she would stay exclusively with him until the bar closed or the guy went to a different bar.   Some guys became lucky, but it was expensive.   If the girl he spent his money on liked him, she would take him to her home to live.

All the girls worked nights, until the bars closed; most of the guys didn't move in with a girl, they just danced and paid for their drinks.   The few guys who wanted the girl exclusively paid the bar for full-time service and moved in with them.   I met a girl who understood, I would only see her on weekends if I wasn't on duty.

Natsumi was a tiny girl, standing four feet ten and weighing around eighty pounds.   She was extremely beautiful, with long black flaxen hair and a very petite body.   At eighteen, she looked to be twelve.   When I first met her at the bar where she worked, I was entranced by her incredible beauty.   For her exclusive company, I bought her drinks and enjoyed with her by dancing, almost every dance.   Dancing with her wasn't easy.   Her head came to just blow my breastplate.   I had to bend at the waist to get my arms around her tiny waist.

As time moved on, Natsumi and I became closer than friends. She lived in a big house with two other girls, who already had boyfriends. Spending weekends with Natsumi wasn't dull.   By buying her time for weekends, she didn't have to work.   On those weekends, we traveled the island.   She showed me where she used to live before being sold to the bar by her father.

The first time I saw Natsumi naked was when I bought her for the weekend.   We took a bus to where she lived.   I was introduced to the others who live there and the guys they lived with.   Compared to the other girls, Natsumi was a miniature doll.

That night, when it was time to go to bed, she locked the door behind us.   In the room, we quickly undressed, then stood and stared at each other.

Natsumi was a natural beauty, very tiny in every sense of the word. As tiny as she was, she had great feminine curves.   With a smile on her face, she climbed into bed.   Just looking at her tiny body was a pleasure. The first time, because of her size, I was afraid I would hurt her.   As it turned out, she wasn't a virgin.

In bed, Natsumi, because of her size, preferred riding on top.   My size made it a little uncomfortable for her to begin with.   The look on her face when she took me let me know she was a little uncomfortable with my size.   Having sex with Natsumi was satisfying.   Not fantastic like with Lana, but very satisfying.

She was addicting to bed.   I spent every weekend with her except when I had duty. When I saw Natsumi the weekend after my duty, she tried to make up for lost time.   I enjoyed every weekend I spent with her.

TWENTY-FIVE

NATSUMI

When I was fifteen, my father, a poor dirt farmer, sold me to the bar for a certain amount of money. It was my choice how I paid that money back, so I could be free.

For the first three years, I worked only as a bar girl, no sex. The guys bought me drinks, for which I get paid a portion of the cost. I loved dancing, so it was easy for me to get the guys to buy me drinks. The men had real drinks, where we would get drinks that looked real, but weren't.

After my third year, I allowed myself to have sex, but only with men who acted and looked nice. At the time, I had only been with two men. I didn't particularly like sex, but it paid better. If I wanted to be free, having sex was the easiest way.

On one particular night, when I saw him walk in, I knew he was a man I wanted to know. He looked older, but he had a lot of muscle and was very handsome. I made myself available.

"Are looking for a girl?" I asked.

"Yes. What are you drinking?"

"I will get your drink when you want it. What would you like?"

"A Tom Collins," he told me, "And whatever you drink."

"What is your name? I'm called Natsumi."

"My name is Bruce.

I could tell Bruce liked what he saw.   Now, all I had to do was find a way to get him for myself."

 For my exclusive company, Bruce bought me drinks and enjoy dancing almost every dance with me.   Dancing with me wasn't easy for him.   My head came to just below his chest.   He had to bend at the waist to get his arm around my waist.

Bruce came every weekend, except when he had a duty.   I stopped having sex with other men, hoping I could win him for myself.   Each time he came to me, we I could tell he wanted to be more than friends. It took me a little more than a month to get him to want me.

One time, he came in and asked me where I lived.

"If you want, I can show you where I live."

"What time do you get off work?"

"Midnight, but you can buy my time."

"Who do I talk to?"

"Come, I will introduce you."

"Are you the man who owns her?"

"I don't own her; she just owes me money."

"I can only get away in weekends. How much would it cost?"

Bruce haggled with the man. When Bruce was satisfied, Bruce paid him.

Natsumi, you are free weekends. Be happy," the man told her.

When I left the bar, I took him to where I catch the bus. It was late Friday night, so I was free for the weekend. Taking the bus, it took ten minutes to get to where I live. When we got there, everyone was there. So, I introduced them to the others.

Once Bruce met my roommates and the boys who lived with them. Wanting to be by myself with him, I took him by the hand and led Bruce to my room.   In the room, before we undressed, we kissed.   He was so tall that O had to stand on tiptoe to reach his mouth.

After that kiss, I was ready for what we came into the room to do. When I saw him naked, I became afraid.   The few men I had been with were not that big down there.

First, I took him to the bathing house.   I washed him.   Even his big penis.   When we were through, we went back to the bedroom.   Climbing onto my bed, I watched him as he climbed in beside me.   To my surprise, he didn't move one me as I expected him to do.

Wrapping his arms around me, he pulled me close, then began kissing and feeling every part of my body.   The feeling I got from him was different than with the other men.   He wanted me to enjoy the act.

When he did move over me, I held my breath, waiting for him to hurt me.   To my surprise, it didn't hurt that much.   I guess it wasn't hurt; it was uncomfortable.   I suffered that first time, but he was so gentle. After that first time, I sort of got used to him.   He never really hurt me, but he was big, which made sex a little difficult.   He was a good man.

On those weekends, when we were together, we traveled the island. I showed where I used to live before I was sold to the bar.   Since I met Bruce, I'm really enjoying life.   I never wanted it to end.

TWENTY-SIX

BRUCE

Compared to the other girls I've seen at the bars, Natsumi was a miniature doll. I began to wonder if Natsumi would always be the way she is when we're alone, or would get Americanized when she gets to the States. Then again, since she really didn't have family per se, would she miss her home country and need to go back now and then.

We spend many hours on the beach. She loved the sand and water. A few nights, I took her to a baseball game. She knew the sport but had never seen one. She would stand and holler and clap when the other people did, but she seemed to enjoy herself.

Time was passing by. I knew the time to say goodbye was near. I had a feeling, my going was going to hurt her more than it would hurt me. Of anything, I will never forget her. Before I leave this island, I'm going to buy her out and help her find a real job.

Buying her out was a little expensive, but she was too good a woman to have to sell herself to make a living. With a real job, she can find some guy worthy of her, whether it's a man from her country or a man from the States.

One week before we left, she had a job in a department store selling.

The day I told Natsumi the Battalion was leaving, she cried. It almost broke my heart to see her so sad, but I wasn't looking for a wife. If I were, Natsumi would have been the perfect girl to bring home to

Mom.   Because of her beauty, I knew someday Natsumi would find some nice guy to marry her, which took some of the hurt away.   I wasn't ready for such a commitment.

We spent our last night together at her house.   It was a bittersweet time.   The next day, our last day in Okinawa, was spent packing.   When it was time to board the plane, I looked back one more time.   So far, my life has been nothing but turmoil.

When we arrived back in the States, all the married guys were happy. I had no one to greet me.   One thing I did correctly was that I passed my test and became a second-class petty office.   That promotion made my life a lot easier.

For the next three months, while back at home base, time moved quickly.   I played a lot of sports and used the pool almost every day.

It was time to go back to Camp Pendleton for training.   My next two deployments were supposed to be to Guam and Hawaii.   But upon my return, I found I had received a new set of orders to Guantanamo Bay, Cuba.

With three weeks before I had to report to Gitmo, I decided to visit home. It had been two years since the last home I had been home. One strong memory made the decision for me.   I couldn't get Lana out of my mind.   I tried to forget her, but I couldn't; she was in my blood.

Knowing two years was a long time for two people, who used to be lovers, to be apart with no communication, is asking much, but I had to try.   The first thing I wanted to do when I got home was call Lana.   She probably wouldn't want to talk to me, and I can't say I blame her.

Finding her old cell phone number in my dresser, I took the chance and called.   I didn't have anything to lose.   Being it has been two years, I felt that when she found out who was calling, she would hang up.   Hell, she has probably married and divorced again.   Even so, I wanted her to know I have been thinking about her.

Dialing her number, I wondered what Lana looked like after two years.   She would be thirty-seven now and most likely be sexy as hell.

"Hello," she said.

"Hi Lana."

"Bruce?"

"The one and only."

"You have a lot of nerve calling me after two years? Did you really think I would wait this long for you to call?"

"No, not really. I just wanted to let you know, even after all these years, you have always been on my mind. I wanted to say hello, even if you didn't want to talk to me."

"Damn, Bruce, you know, you will always be the main part of my life. Actually, you still are. You always will be, but I'm now dating a nice man, and he doesn't deserve to be hurt."

"Well, I'm happy for you. You deserve a good guy in your life. I understand, and I am very happy that you would still want to talk to me."

There was a slight hesitation on her end of the line. I thought she was going to hang up. Just about to hang up, I hesitated long enough to hear her speak.

TWENTY-SEVEN

BRUCE

"Where are you?" she asked

"At my parents' home in Madison."

"How long will you be home?"

"I have three weeks before I have to report to Cuba."

"Damn you, Bruce," she cried, "You know, I have never forgotten you. The guy I'm dating now is nice and generous, but he isn't you."

"Like I said, as long as you are happy, I'm happy for you."

"I'm as happy as I can be, with you not in my life," she sighed, "Damn you, Bruce. You're in my blood. I know this is stupid and I shouldn't do this, but if you want me to, I will come down Saturday and spend the night."

"That would be great. I will love to see you again."

"I can't wait to see you," she cried.

"Should I get a room?"

"Hell yes. I'm not driving all that way just to talk."

"Did you move?"

"Yes, I live sixty miles from where I used to live. I'll bring you up to date when I see you."

"I still love you, Lana?"

"I still love you, too," she said and hung up.

Hanging up, I couldn't help but smile. It was hard to believe Lana would actually come to see him after all these years. After hanging up, I still had two days before Saturday. To make sure we had the room when she came, I rented our room for that Saturday for the night. It happened to be the same room Lana and I had use before.

Saturday came, and I was becoming anxious to see her again. Knowing Lana, she would be here in a couple of hours. Not wanting to miss her, I laid on the bed for a nap. It wasn't until I felt the bed sag, I opened my eyes.

I was stunned to find Lana lying on the bed next to me. I never heard her come in, which sort of scared me. I'm not much of a heavy sleeper.

Rolling to face her, I opened my arms.

"Hi," she said.

Moving into my embrace, she planted a hot kiss on my lips. Her kiss was just as I remembered. Soft and hot.

"Hi yourself," I said, responding.

That was the beginning. How we got out of our clothes and into our hot embrace is still unsolved. After a reminder of what we have been missing for these last two years, we remained in bed the entire day. Late that night, with hunger setting in, we went out to dinner. It was great to be with her like this again.

Our meal was something we both needed after such a workout. The meal was a prelude of what was to come. Minutes later, we headed back to bed. It was as if it was our first time. Exhaustion put us to sleep.

It was almost noon Sunday when we awoke. Being together was great. So as to really enjoy each other, we took a leisurely ride.

She had changed her mind; she was staying Sunday night. Later that night, I awoke to find Lana crying. Taking her into my arms, I let her vent. Early the next morning, we talked about the last two years. I didn't have to tell her everything; she knew. She knew I hadn't been celibate.

"Mike, the guy I'm dating, is ten years older than me and wants me to marry him. He has two daughters, a few years older than my daughters.

"How old are your daughters now?"

"Seventeen and fourteen. My oldest will be going to college next year."

"What about the two other girls in your new family?"

"They are both married and have children of their own."

"So, it will be just you, him, and your youngest daughter?" I asked.

"Yeah, and I now realize I haven't learned a thing."

"What are you talking about?"

"My fiancée doesn't travel a lot, but then again, he is a devout workaholic."

"So, things really haven't changed."

"No. I could have gone with you and been happy when you did come home from your deployments."

"It's not too late," I told her.

"You would still take me as I am?"

"Hell yes. Any place, any time."

"I'm flattered, but I have to use common sense. As much as I love you and always will, you are gone longer and more often than Mike is."

"He is a lucky guy."

She chuckled.

"After this weekend, you should know I will come flying to you whenever you are home, unless you get married," she told me.

"Marriage is not in the books for me, Lana. As much as I travel, it wouldn't be fair to whoever she would be."

"Yet you would marry me?" she said.

"You are my special angel."

"Damn you, Bruce," she began to cry.

"What's wrong now?" I asked.

"I won't be able to see you again before you go."

"Just be thankful we had these two nights together."

"I am thankful, but leaving you is always the hardest thing I have to do. Loving a man more than the man you're going to marry is terrible."

"I'm going to miss you, too, Lana, more than you realize."

"I already miss you and you are still with me," she said, "But from this time on, I will have some great memories to take with me."

"Are you hurting?" I asked her.

"I'm sore again. Your size is so big. You are the only man that always makes me feel sore."

After Lana left, I drove home in a funky mood. Knowing how we felt toward each other only made not seeing her much more difficult. When I got home, my parents were waiting.

"Don't tell me," Mom said, "You were with her again."

"Yes. But she is getting married again."

"I didn't know she was divorced," Mom said.

"She got divorced before I left two years ago."

"If that is the case, why didn't you two get together?"

"She didn't like the idea I would be gone nine months every year."

"Then may this be for the best then," Mom said.

TWENTY-EIGHT

LANA

I was just about to leave the house for shopping when the phone rang.

"Hello," she said

"Hi Lana."

"Bruce?"

"The one and only."

"You have a lot of nerve calling me after two years? Did you really think I would wait this long for you to call?" Did you think I would wait that long for you?"

Just hearing his voice sent old memories through me. I was going to act as if I was pissed, because I am, but hearing his voice changed all that. Even after all this time, I was hoping he would want to see me again.

"No, not really," he said, "I just wanted to let you know, even after all these years, you have always been on my mind. I wanted to say hello, even if you didn't want to talk to me."

Hearing him say those words made me want him again. That was something that hasn't happened to me since the last time we had been together. Those words made me say something I didn't want to say, something I shouldn't have said.

"Bruce, you were a main part of my life. Actually, you still are and always will be, but I'm dating a nice man now and don't want to hurt him."

"I understand. I just wanted to touch bases."

Right then, I knew I couldn't let him get away without seeing him again. I tried not to say what I was thinking, but I couldn't stop myself.

"Where are you?" I asked

"At my parents' home in Madison."

"How long are you home for?"

"I have two weeks before I have to head to Cuba."

"Damn you, Bruce," I groaned.

My mind and body were betraying me. Mike is a good lover, but he just doesn't do for me what Bruce does. Just knowing how disparately I wanted to feel him inside my body one more time. I was stupid when I said the words.

"You know, I have never forgotten you," I told him, "The guy I'm dating now is nice and generous, but he isn't you."

"I'm happy for you, as long as you are happy," Bruce said.

"I'm as happy as I can be, with you not in my life," I sighed, "Damn you. I know this is stupid and I shouldn't do this, but if you still want me, I will come down this Saturday and spend the night."

"You should know I would love to see you again," he told me, "Should I get a room?"

"Hell yes," I cried, "I'm not driving all that way just to talk."

Just thinking of being with him this weekend has made me wet. I could actually feel him inside me doing things to me that no man has ever done.

"Did you move?" he asked.

"Yes, I live sixty miles from where I used to live. I'll bring you up to date when I see you."

Hanging up, I smiled. Saturday is a long time away, and I could hardly wait. Then Mike called.

"Lana, I have to go on a business trip for a few days. I should be home by Tuesday."

"Then I'm going to spend my time at the beach," I told him. This was perfect. He wouldn't call and find me gone. If he calls, I'll be there to talk to him.

"Have fun, see you when I get home."

Real early Saturday morning, I hurriedly climbed into her car. Feeling totally anxious, I couldn't get there fast enough. As soon as I got my daughters off to school, I was ready for the trip.

"I'll be gone until Tuesday," I told my daughters, "I need some time to myself."

On the road, time flew. My body couldn't wait for the satisfaction I knew I was going to get. An hour and a half later, thirty minutes less than it really took, I pulled into the parking area. Out of the corner of my eye, I saw his car. Pulling into the only space left, next to his, I couldn't get out of the car fast enough. My heart was beating so wildly that I thought I would faint.

Making the long walk from the car to the door, which was about thirty steps, made my pulse quicken. Finally making the long walk to the door that led me to surmountable pleasure, I was about to knock when the door moved. To my surprise, the door was partially open. Pushing it all the way open, I froze.

Bruce was lying on the bed, completely naked, asleep. Not wanting to wake him yet, I entered the room, closed and locked the door. Then, quickly undressing, I lay next to him on the bed. After two years, I wasn't too sure I would turn him on like I used to. Time has made changes to my body and looks.

Nevertheless, this opportunity only came once in my lifetime. Now on the bed with him, I just lay beside him, admiring his physique. It wasn't until he opened his eyes that I touched him.

"Hi," she said.

"Hi yourself," he responded.

Unable to hold off any longer, I went into his embrace. Planting a warm, hot kiss on his lips ignited me instantly. My kiss must have ignited him as quickly. Bruce came at me like he did the first time. I couldn't help but remember those three days. He was like a machine. He drove himself into me three times. Even as sore as he made me, it's sad to say, that day didn't seem enough for me. The first time, I couldn't contain myself. The pace was fast and furious.

This time was no different. I remained in bed with him the whole day. It was exhausting, but oh so worth it, even if he still made me sore. Not only did I feel the exhaustion again, but I found I was sore all over again. I had little trouble remembering how quick he was to recover. As sore as I was, I wasn't going to let this opportunity slip by.

Five minutes later, I couldn't contain the moan that escaped me as he entered me a second time. Later that night, with a hunger for him, but needing a rest, we took the time to go out to dinner.

As strange as it was, before our meal was consumed, I was ready for dessert. I didn't care how sore I was; I couldn't wait to get back to bed. Hell, when he's gone, I'll be wishing I went with him. After that, our time tonight, exhaustion put us to sleep.

It was almost noon Sunday when I awoke. Just being with him like this again made my day perfect. When he awoke, all I had to do was look at him. A few minutes later, we took one more leisurely ride. Never in her life had I ever wanted sex so often as I did now.

That night, after Bruce fell asleep, I cried. It made me sad to know that tonight would be my last time with him. God only knows how long that will be before the next time. It was ridiculous for a woman my age to be in love with a man so much younger.

Early the next morning, we talked about the last two years we had been apart. I was sure Bruce was leaving off the woman he had been spending all his time with. There was no way a man like him could stay celibate for two years.

On the other hand, Mike, the guy I'm dating, is ten years older than me. He has even asked me to marry him and has two daughters of his own, a few years older than my daughters.

"So, it will be just me, him, and my youngest daughter after we are married.

"After this weekend, I now realize I haven't learned a thing," I told Bruce.

"What are you talking about?"

"My fiancée is a workaholic."

"So, things haven't changed."

"No. I could have gone with you and been happy when you did come home from your deployments."

"It's not too late," Bruce told me.

"You would still take me as I am?" I asked.

"Hell yes. Any place, any time."

"I'm flattered, but I have to use common sense. As much as I love you and always will, you are gone longer and more often than Mike is."

"He is a lucky guy."

I chuckled, then said, "After this weekend, you should know I will come flying to you whenever you are home, unless you get married."

"Marriage is not in the books for me. As much as I travel, it wouldn't be fair to whoever she would be."

"Yet you would marry me?" I spoke.

"You are my special angel."

"Damn you, Bruce," I began crying.

"What is wrong now?" he asked.

"Leaving you is always the hardest thing I have to do. Loving a man more than the man I'm getting married to is terrible."

"I'm going to miss you, too, Lana, more than you realize."

"I already miss you and you are still with me," I told him, "But from this time on, I will have some great memories to take with me."

"Are you hurting?" he asked.

"Yes, I'm sore again. Your size is sort of big for me. You are the only man that has ever made me feel sore."

TWENTY-NINE

BRUCE

The day before my leave was over, I went to Andrews Air Force Base in New Jersey, where I was to catch my flight to Cuba. While waiting for my flight, I met a few other guys from different departments of the military, heading to the same place. We talked about where we have been and what we have been doing.

Arriving in Gitmo, the moment I stepped off the plane, my body became soaked with sweat. Christ, another hot box, I thought. The battalion had sent a drive for me. As the driver drove through the base, I was amazed at how huge the base was. It seemed as big as a city in the States, with everything a person could want to do or want.

Seven miles later, the driver pulled into the personnel office. Handing over my orders, I was taken to the Charlie Company Office. Being I joined the battalion after it deployed, I was put on a crew laying chain-link fence for an ammo dump. By the time I joined the crew, all the holes were already dug. Once the poles were sealed in place with concrete, the last thing to do would be to string the chain length to the poles.

Nights were spent drinking and gambling for most of the men. I never indulged, putting me on the outs with my peers. I preferred reading, playing chess, and playing sports. Once in a while, I walked the mile to the beach.

The main beach was a favorite place for families to go. Cabanas offered families shade and a place to store what their belongings while they were swimming. Several cabanas were spread around the beach area. A huge coral reef surrounded the swimming area to keep out big, menacing fish.

Snorkeling was a favorite for a lot of the people. The world of diving is beautiful and exciting. Those who snorkel had a small hole in the reef at high tide to swim through. That hole closed after a few hours. Once the water went below the hole, the opening would disappear. Swimmers caught on the outside would have no choice but to crawl over the coral reef. Sea Urchins and sharp coral made the return trip very dangerous and difficult.

After a dip, I liked to explore the coral rim. Trolling the edge could be dangerous. One bad step and a person could fall over thirty feet into the water, and it could be fatal. One never knew how deep the water was just over the edge.

Naturally curious, I love to explore. Not afraid of the rim, I would walk to see what I could see. On one exploring mission, I came upon a small sandy beach. I happened to find the beach after a twenty-minute walk on the corral ledge. A person would never find the beach unless he were exploring.

Standing on the edge, looking down, I saw what looked like a small winding path leading to the beach below. Curious, I followed the path. It led through the coral to the sandy beach below. Letting my curiosity get the better of me, I cautiously took the tiny path down to the small beach.

The beach was so hidden, it definitely wasn't a place young kids should never go, let alone curious people like me. Hoping I wouldn't fall, I wound my way down the path.

On the beach, a slight breeze blowing in from the sea made the beach somewhat bearable. With curiosity getting the better of me, I decided to explore a little further. It was low tide, so I waded out waist-deep into the water. With the bottom being sandy, I was able to search.

During my search, I discovered a small ledge leading along at the bottom of the coral reef. As it was, it was barely visible just below the water. The ledge followed along the base of the wall. At high tide, the ledge would never be seen.

Following a ledge, as I rounded a corner, a short distance away, I saw what looked like a cave, carved into the wall. Taking my time, to be sure I didn't slip, I waded to where the opening was. From the marking of the water leaves, the cave opening would be covered at high tide.

Making it to the entrance, I peered inside. The inside was a small, shallow room with a sandy floor and a small pool of water near the entrance. Further back, though it was sort of dark, it looked to be a sandy beach and dry. The entrance to the cave wasn't too difficult to climb into.

Finding the interior of the cave cooler than outside, I sat in the sand with my feet in the small warm puddle. As quiet as it was inside, the slightest noise could be heard from outside. That odd sound alerted me.

I didn't like the idea of being caught on the inside, but since there was only one way in and one way out, I was stuck, and that made me nervous.

THIRTY

BRUCE

Going into a corner where I would be somewhat protected from sight, I could use the surprise advantage on whoever it was. I prepared myself for whatever as I stared at the opening. Hearing the movement of the water, I just knew whoever it was headed for the entrance.

As the person reached the opening, a small, dark hand grasped the edge of the opening. With a grunt, a tiny female body slid inside. She didn't see me. When she finally saw me in the corner, her first reaction was to back away.

"Oh, I'm sorry," she said, in surprise, "I didn't know anyone else knew of this place."

Quickly moving from the shadow of the corner, I confronted her.

"Don't be sorry. Since you seem to know this place, stay. I just happened to find this place a few minutes ago."

When she didn't turn to run, as I thought she might, she remained planter in her footsteps. For just a moment, she looked as if she were studying my face and body. After another few moments, a cute smile spread across her face.

"Aren't you the guy who runs the pool?" she asked.

"Yes."

"Hi, my name is Delores," she said.

She extended her tiny hand to me. When I took her hand, she sighed. Delores was a beauty. She stood about five feet tall. This black girl was not only pretty, she had a petite figure, to go along with a pretty smile. Her smile put me at ease. Her hair was cut short and shaped in an Afro. Her very pretty milk chocolate face glistened from the water.

"I'm Bruce," I told her.

She held onto my hand longer than necessary.

"Are you still in high school or first year of college?"

"I just graduated high school and will be starting college in the fall," she said.

Still holding my hand, her grip seemed to get tighter.

"Where are you from?" she asked.

"My home state is Connecticut. How about you?"

"My family is from Brooklyn."

"Since you are starting college, I'd say you were eighteen."

"I'll be eighteen in two months. How old are you?"

"I'm twenty-five."

"That's only seven years older than me."

The way she was looking at me and saying what she told me, she was sizing me up. Standing, perhaps a foot taller than her, she looked like a real live doll. Being Delores was standing so close to me, her eyes took in everything about me. She started by gazing at my short blond hair, then slowly let her eyes travel downward.

Her eyes widened as they landed on my crotch. My crotch was very noticeable, since I had become hard just being this close to her. Seeing the girl's stare, to go along with her sexy little body, was all it took for me to be hard.

"I've never dated a white guy before," she said, in a sexy voice, "None of the guys I've dated are as old as you either."

"Then we are even," I said, staring at her, "I've never been out with a black girl as sexy as you either."

"How long are you here for?" she asked.

"Eight more months," I told her.

"And you haven't found a girlfriend yet?"

"No," I said, shaking my head, "What about you? When do you go back to school?"

"I have six weeks left," she said.

"And you don't have any boyfriends yet?"

She laughed.

"It isn't I haven't found a boyfriend yet," she said with a grin, "I just haven't found one that has me interested until now."

"In that case," I said, "Maybe you and I can enjoy each other now and then."

"I like the sound of that," she said, "Actually, I was hoping to suggest that."

Standing as close to her as I was and hearing what she was saying, I didn't care how old she was; I had to go for it. Delores might be a little young for me, but she was all but asking for it. The look in her eyes told me what she wanted. With her beauty drawing me to her, I the chance and took the imitative.

THIRTY-ONE

Placing my hands on her slim hips, I pulled her against me. With a sigh, she came willingly. Wrapping her arms around my neck, she had to stand on tip-toe for the kiss. As I pulled her against me, she pressed her hips firmly against me. As I tasted her soft, sweet lips, she quickly invaded my mouth with her tongue. As we played tongue tag, she quickly lost all her control.

"Ooooh," she moaned.

"Damn, you taste good," I told her.

"I like the way you kiss, too," she moaned.

Without any hesitation, our kisses and fondling quickly became passionate. I slid my hands down her tiny body. Finding the soft, solid cheeks of her generous bottom, I cupped them. Her hands did one better. She slid her hands inside my bathing suit, quickly grabbing my erection.

Instantly, she sagged to the sand. Pulling me down with her, we lay in the sand. Our kisses became bolder. Then, coming up for air, which lasted just a moment, we managed to strip down naked.

Laying naked in the sand, she made herself ready for me. Kneeling between her thighs, I felt her hand direct me. Just as I penetrated her, a freezing wave broke through the opening, drenching our hot bodies.

"Holly shit," I cried, as I pulled out.

"Oh damn, why now? Put it back in," she cried, "I think we have time to finish."

Penetrating one more time, we rode the few waves coming through the hole.   Finished, we scrambled back into our suits.   Quickly vacating the cave, we moved into open water.   Grasping tightly to her hand, I pulled her with me.

"You don't have to do this," she said, "I can swim."

"I don't doubt that for a minute," I told her, "But I want to be sure.

Pulling her to within a few feet of the beach, the waves didn't seem as rough there.

"Can you come to the beach tomorrow?" she asked.

"My only free day is Sunday.   I work from sunup to sundown six days a week."

"I have to wait a whole week?" she gasped.

"We both do, and it won't be any easy for me either.   Getting started and finishing so fast is hell."

"There has to be a way we can satisfy our needs right now," she said.

Swiftly coming back into my arms, she kissed me harder.   It didn't take much for her to regenerate my passion.   Not daring to be caught by prying eyes, we quickly separated.

"That wasn't enough," she cried.

Agreeing with her, I grabbed her again.   Moaning wildly, she jumped onto me.   Winding her legs around my waist, I could feel her heat pressing against my hardness.   Remembering how it felt to be inside her, even for so short a time, was more than I could take.

"Damn," I groaned, "Come on."

With Delores clinging to me, I rushed back into the water.   It wasn't high tide yet, and there was one place along the ledge that would be safe. I had to hole her up as I made my way to the small nook I remember seeing.

With the water not quite up to my armpits and with Delores still with legs around, I made it to the nook.

In the heat of the moment, I pushed my suit down to just below my crotch, hoping the force of the water wouldn't float my suit away. Quickly, I managed to uncover her vagina. Hanging on tightly to her lush bottom, I pushed my hardness against her. With no wasted motion, her hand snaked between us.

Grasping my hardness, it was evident she wasn't to be denied. That was all she needed. With a wild cry, she tightened her legs around my waist. That movement forced me to sink deep into her heat.

The feel of her enveloping my hardness, into her soft womanhood, made him groan with extreme pleasure. Unable to hold back, I began to thrust wildly into her warm, tightness. Her head fell back as she unleashed an animistic cry.

"Jesus, fuck me harder," she cried.

In the heat of the moment, I didn't waste any time. My thrusts became quick and hard. She responded by moving her hips to match my every thrust. Our passions rose and ended quickly when our long cries of satisfaction were released.

"I'm going to come," I told her.

"Come inside me," she moaned.

Moments later, Delores was swimming back to the beach as I took the time to pull my bathing suit back into place. Finished, I followed her. She was standing in the sand, unable to control herself. The moment I got there, she kissed me, one last time, before parting.

THIRTY-TWO

DELORES

I t was a hot day, and I was horny as hell. The guy I have been dating is a dud. His attempts at sex were childless. All he could think of was getting his rocks off. He seemed to forget there was a woman who needed as much satisfaction as he does.

He called today, and I told him I was busy. I really wasn't, but I didn't need that kind of relationship. Thinking as I was, I knew if I wanted good sex, I was going to have to find it elsewhere.

Maybe a good walk and a swim in the ocean was what I needed. We didn't live far from the beach, but if I went there, Perry might come down, and I didn't need that.

When I got to the beach, I decided to go to my favorite place. Nobody knows about the place, so I would have time to myself. When I got to the beach, I took the dirt trail that led to a beach, maybe a mile away. My place was probably half the distance.

Reaching the quiet beach, I slowly made my way down the path to the sandy beach. The tide was coming in, but I had plenty of time to get to my cave before the tide drove me out.

Finding the ledge at the bottom of the coral, I made my way to my cave. Swinging my body into the opening, then seeing something move from the corner, scared me.

"Oh, I'm sorry," I cried, in surprise, "I didn't know anyone else knew of this place."

Quickly moving from the corner, a white guy confronted me.

"Don't be sorry. Since you seem to know this place, stay. I just happened to find this place a few minutes ago."

Even after a quick glance, for some reason, I didn't feel any fear, so I didn't run. Instead, I began studying his face and body. After another few moments, liking what I was seeing, I gave him a cute smile.

"Hi, my name is Delores," I said.

Extending my hand, when he took it, all I could do was sigh. From the look on his face, I could see he liked what he was seeing.

"I'm Bruce," he said.

Suddenly wanting to know him better, I held onto his hand longer than necessary.

"Are you still in high school or first year of college?"

"I just graduated high school and will be starting college in the fall," I said.

Still holding his hand, I gripped him tighter.

"Where are you from?" she asked.

"My home state is Connecticut. How about you?"

"My family is from Brooklyn."

"Since you are starting college, I'd say you were eighteen."

"I'll be eighteen in two months. How old are you?"

"I'm twenty-five."

"That's only seven years older than me."

The way I looked at him told him I was sizing me up. He stood perhaps a foot taller than me. Wanting to see what he would do, I made sure I was standing very close to him.   Starting with his eyes, let my eyes travel downward.   When they landed on his crotch, I noticed he was already in the mood.

"I've never dated a white guy before," I said, in a sexy voice, "None of the guys I've dated were as old as you either."

"Then we are even," he said, staring at me, "I've never been out with a black girl, as sexy as you either."

"How long are you here for?" I asked.

"Eight more months," he told me.

"And you haven't found a girlfriend yet?"

"No," he said, "What about you?   When do you go back to school?"

"I have six weeks left," I said.

"And you don't have any boyfriends yet?"

I laughed, "It isn't I haven't found a boyfriend yet," I said, "I just haven't found one that has me interested, until now."

"In that case," he said, "Maybe you and I can enjoy each other now and then."

"I like the sound of that," I said, "Actually, I was hoping you would suggest that."

Standing so close to me, I didn't care how old he was. When he his hands grabbed my hips and pulled me against him.   I came willingly. Wrapping my arms around his neck and standing on tip-toe, he kissed me.   Now, pressing my hips against him, his lips met mine.   I quickly invaded his mouth with my tongue.

"Ooooh," I moaned.

"Damn, you taste good," he said.

"I like the way you kiss, too," I moaned.

With no hesitation, he kissed me and ran his hands down my body. As he cupped my bottom, I slid my hand inside his suit. Grabbing his erection, I sagged to the sand, pulling him with me. Laying in the sand, his kisses had me going. We came up for air, for just a moment, somehow managing to get naked.

Laying naked in the sand, I opened my thighs. With him kneeling between them, I placed him where I wanted him. As he penetrated me, a freezing wave broke through the opening, drenching our bodies.

"Holly shit," he cried, pulling out.

"Oh damn, why now? Put it back in," I cried, "I think we have time to finish."

Penetrating me one again, we rode the few waves, as he finished quickly. We scrambled back into our suits, then vacated the cave. In open water, he grasped my hand tightly, pulling me with him.

"You don't have to do this," I said, "I can swim."

"I don't doubt that for a minute," he said, "But I want to be sure."

When we got near the beach, the waves seemed slower.

"Can you come to the beach tomorrow?" I asked.

"My only free day is Sunday. I work from sunup to sundown six days a week."

"I have to wait a whole week?" I gasped.

"We both do, and it won't be any easy for me either. Getting started and finishing so fast is hell."

"There has to be a way we can satisfy our needs right now," she said.

Swiftly coming back into his arms, I kissed him harder. It didn't take me long to regenerate his passion again. Not daring to be caught by prying eyes, we quickly separated.

"That wasn't enough," I cried.

Agreeing with me, he grabbed me again.   Moaning wildly, I jumped on him, winding my legs around his waist.   I could feel his hardness pressing against my covered vagina.

"Damn," he groaned, "Come on."

With me clinging to him, he rushed back into the water.   We made it back to the ledge.   Holding me up, he somehow managed to uncover my vagina.   Holding on tightly, I snaked my hand between us.   Grasping his erection, with a wild cry, I tightened my legs around him.   Feeling him sink deep into me.

"Jesus, fuck me harder," she cried.

"I'm going to come," he told me.

"Come inside me," she moaned.

Moments later, I swam back to the beach.   After Bruce had his bathing suit back in place, he followed me.   Standing in the sand, barely unable to control myself, I kissed him one last time before parting.

Every Sunday, for the next six weeks, before I had to leave for school, Bruce and I slaked our lust and took out our frustrations at the beach. Out of the six weeks, they were able to use the cave almost full-time. The last day we spent together, we waited until the last second before vacating the cave.

"I hope you were on the pill, Dee," Bruce said.

"It's a little late to worry about that now, but you should be safe," I said, kissing him.

After our last kiss, I said, "I'm going to miss this dumb cave."

"Dee, I'm going to miss you.   I hope you have a good life, get your education, and marry some nice guy who deserves you."

"I'm going to miss you too, Bruce," I said, clinging to him, "I have grown quite fond of you.

"I've become very fond of you, too, Dee. If you weren't going to school and we had more time together, I think we could have gotten closer."

I looked down, ashamed of my attitude, then said, "My parents are strictly against interracial marriages."

"How do you feel about interracial marriages?" he asked.

"With you, I could go for it, but I have to honor my parents' wishes."

"I guess this is it then," he said sadly.

"I'm afraid so, but I will never forget you or the times we had together," I said.

For the rest of his tour, Bruce concentrated on his work and studies. He wanted to make a higher rank before this deployment was over. Hard work gave him his promotion and a new set of orders. Going back to Hueneme for shore duty was perfect.

THIRTY-THREE

BRUCE

Before heading to California, I decided to take a couple of weeks at home. This was the first time Lana ever turned me down. Lana had just married Mike and wanted to remain faithful to him. We did talk for a time before hanging up.

Lana's life has undergone a few changes. Her oldest daughter, who was now nineteen and was supposed to college, had gotten pregnant and married her high school sweetheart. Her youngest daughter, now sixteen, was now a junior in high school. Lana wanted to give her youngest daughter more quality time than she did with her eldest daughter.

The time wasn't wasted; I spent the entire two weeks with my parents, which made my mom extremely happy. Especially, now that I wasn't seeing the married woman any longer. My two weeks of complete leisure at home ended quickly. On my flight to California, I had plenty of time to think.

My tour at Hueneme was for two years. Not wanting to live on base, I rented a nice apartment in town close to the base. After moving in, I was able to get a good night's sleep. No more snores to keep me awake.

Leaving early every morning for the base and not returning until dark, I never got to meet any of my neighbors. It wasn't until I got some free time that things began to change. It was Friday evening, and I had the weekend off. With free time on my hands, I decided to relax in the hot tub. Being it was my first time, I was lucky that there wasn't anyone there. It seemed strange to have no one at the swimming pool or relaxing in a lounge.

Finally, alone where I could relax, I sauntered to the hot tub. Stepping in, the feel of the hot water was a joy. Sitting near a jet, to let the jets pound on my sore muscles, I was able to relax for the first time in a long time. Soaking up this hot water, with these sore muscles, I was able to scrunch down, lay my head back, and close my eyes.

A sudden noise made my eyes pop open. My uninterrupted time was over. A moment later, a cute redhead came around the corner. I watched as she slid into the Jacuzzi across from me. She was definitely a looker. I didn't say anything, waiting for her to break the silence.

"Hi, I'm Julia Parker," she said, "I haven't seen you before. Are you new to the place?"

"I've been living here about a week."

A beautiful smile covered her pretty face. Her smile made me return that smile. Guessing her age to be eighteen or nineteen, I looked at her hands. She was wearing rings.

"I'm Bruce Benson."

"It is nice to meet you, Bruce. Which room is yours?"

"I live on the first floor," I told her.

"Oh, as you can see, I am married. My husband and I live on the second floor."

"Where is he now?"

"He is in the military. He comes home every night, except when he has duty."

For a married woman, she was giving me more information than I needed to know. I guessed she was just being friendly, but she wanted me to know her status.

"How long has your husband been in?" Bruce asked.

"A little over a year now.   He is waiting for permanent orders."

Having been in the Jacuzzi so long, I was well past my limit. Excusing myself, I climbed out.

"I think it's time for me to take a dip," I told her.

No sooner had I left the tub when I noticed Julia had followed me. Instead of lying on a lounge, I walked to the small board.   Again, she followed me.   Not only did she have a great body, but she also had dexterity.   The girl impressed me with the way she handled herself.

After a few dives, I left the pool to lay on a lounge.   Acting as if she were with me, Julia followed me as she had both times before.   Taking the lounge next to mine, I couldn't help but watch her bodily movements. As always, I automatically I wondered what she would be like in bed. Around noon, Julia disappeared.

Feeling lost and tired, I retired early.

THIRTY-FOUR

BRUCE

The next day, she came back with a man in tow. The way she was acting, I assumed he was her husband. The guy wasn't very tall and was very skinny. Light brown hair covered his almost bald head, and he was needing a shave, which made him look scruffy. The guy wasn't at all what I would have pictured him to look like.

Before Julia brought her husband over to introduce him, a cute little blond walk over to meet them. Immediately, Julia hugged the girl. Julia's husband all but ignored the girl. Almost immediately, all three came in my direction. For a moment, I didn't know what to expect. Why was Julia coming to me? I had just met her the day before.

"Bruce, I want you to meet my husband, Henry, and my best friend, Sally."

Standing, I offered Henry my hand.

"Hi Henry," I said.

Henry's refusal to shake my hand didn't sit well with me. So I turned my attention to the young girl and extended my hand to her instead.

"Hi, Bruce," Sally said warmly.

"Who is this guy?" Henry asked.

"I told you, Henry. I met Bruce here yesterday, here at the pool," Julia stated, "and since Sally is single, I thought maybe the two of them would like to date."

The moment I was introduced to Henry, something about Henry put me on edge. I didn't like people who reminded me of a 'know-it-all all jerk'. Immediately, I felt sorry for Julia. She was a genuinely warm, likable person. In a way, I was glad I didn't have anything to do with the guy.

Sally, on the other hand, was as cute as a button. As tiny as she was, it was difficult for me to guess her age. Her golden blond hair hung loosely around her slender shoulders. Just looking at her, I knew I would probably never have asked her out, but seeing Julia put me in such an awkward position, and not wanting to hurt the girl, I felt I had to ask her out.

"Do you mind me asking your age?" I asked, "I want to be sure I'm not breaking any rules."

She laughed.

"I understand," she said, "I'm eighteen."

Sally impressed me. She looked to be in her early teens, but because of the way she acted, I took her at her word. Besides being pretty, Sally seemed to have a great sense of humor. Then I remembered Delores. I took a chance with her, and she was only seventeen at the time.

That evening everyone the four of us went to a bar. Knowing Sally was too young to drink, I ordered soft drinks for her and I. Henry had to be the exception. Getting Sally on the dance floor was easy. I found Sally loved to dance, and she was a great dance partner. Henry, on the other hand, turned out to be a wallflower. Julia's face and body language told me she was very disappointed when Henry wouldn't ask her to dance.

"Sally, would you mind if I asked Julia to dance?"

"No. Being her husband is ignoring her, I was going to suggest you do that," Sally said.

After bringing Sally back to the table, we sat for a while and sipped our drinks. When I was sure she was comfortable and the music started, I walked over to Henry.

"Would you mind if I asked your wife to dance?" I asked.

Henry just sat there, like a lump on a log, staring at me.

"I'd love to dance with you," Julia cut in.

On the floor, we dance in the old-fashioned way, hardly touching. Even so, with her in my arms, it felt like we flying. That one dance I had with Julia made her husband come unglued. Instantly feeling sorry for Sally, who I know had to be embarrassed, I stayed strictly with Sally the rest of the night.

It was obvious Henry was about to make an ass of himself. Jealousy was always a deal-breaker. His attitude and temper had him act childishly, and that made Julia furious. Acting like a little kid, Henry pitched a major fit. That started an argument, but the argument didn't last long. It ended with Henry storming from the place.

After Henry left, Julia just sat looking into space, bewildered. Both Sally and I felt sorry for her. With Henry gone, Sally suggested I give Julia another dance.

"Bruce, now that her husband is gone, why don't you ask Julia to dance again?"

Understanding where Sally was coming from, I did as Sally suggested and went to Julia.

"Would you like to dance one last time?" I asked Julia.

"I would love to," she said.

It was obvious her feelings had been hurt. Tears were rimming her eyes. She had all she could do not to break down and cry. When I got her on the floor, Julia melted into my arms, unlike during our first dance.

Holding Julia closer was so much more comfortable and nicer than trying to get comfortable with Sally.

"What is going to happen when you get home?" I asked.

"I have no idea," Julia said, "I guess inviting you to be with Sally didn't sit well with Henry."

"I gathered that. Does he think there is something going on between you and me?"

"Well, he would be wrong. But in defense of you, if I were single, that would be a different story. But as it is, I am married and you are with Sally."

For a while, we remained quiet as we continued moving slowly around the floor.

"To be honest with you," Bruce said, "Sally is a great gal, but she isn't my type. Maybe I shouldn't say this, but you are more my type."

"Me?" Looking up at me, her eyes said one thing, her mouth another.

"What is wrong with Sally? She is tiny, pretty, and smart. There are lot of guys who would love to go out with her."

"What I feel towards a woman goes further than skin deep. You're not only outwardly beautiful, you also have charisma. You feel for people, not just yourself, not like your husband."

"In defense of Henry, he can be a great guy," Julia said, "His jealousy is his downfall."

"That doesn't give him the right to treat you as he did."

"He loves me and is just trying to protect me."

"What I see is," I hesitated, "The person he loves is himself, and he's selfish. He hates the idea of wanting anyone. He thinks he owns you."

THIRTY-FIVE

BRUCE

Dropping Julia at her home first, I then drove Sally to her place. Arriving at where Sally lived, she didn't get right out, but turned in her seat to look at me.

"I had a wonderful time tonight, Bruce. Would you like to come up for a nightcap?" she asked.

"Sure."

After parking, to show her I had a good time, I took her hand as we made our way to her apartment.

"You're a great guy, Bruce, and I had a great time."

"You are a great gal, too, Sally. You know how to treat a guy."

"How did I give you such a nice time?" she asked.

"Just being you was nice."

"I'll take that as a compliment."

"It was meant to be," I told her.

Once inside her apartment, she looked at me sheepishly.

"Actually, I lied," she said, "I didn't have anything to drink. I asked you to come in so I can spend more time with you."

"I really didn't need anything to drink anyway," I told her.

"Do you and Julia have anything going?" she asked suddenly.

"No, Julia and I are just friends. Why do you ask?"

"I asked because if you two had something going, I wouldn't want to interfere."

"Why would you think we had something going?"

"I can see how the two of you act around each other."

"To be honest, I wasn't aware of doing anything special," I said.

"Then I'm going to be honest with you," she said shyly, "Being with you makes me want more. Being in your arms got me wildly turned on.

"Sally I."

"Let me finish," she said, holding up a hand, "I've had sex just one time in my life. It wasn't very satisfying. Now, I need to know, no, I want to know my true feelings about sex."

"Are you're asking me to spend the night?"

"Yes," she said, "I need desperately to know what real sex is like."

"Sally, you're a beautiful woman and could have your pick of any guy you want."

"The only boys I know are my age, or a year older. None of them fit the image I want. Now, I know you are a few years older than me, but your experience is what I want and need."

"Are you sure this is what you want to do?"

"Just saying those words to you has cost me a lot. Just to get up the nerve to tell you how I feel, makes me feel..."

"Whatever you feel would be wrong. I am flattered you have asked. Now, I want to know if you are really sure you want to do this? I would be honored to spend the night with you, but I have to be honest with you. I'm not in the market for a wife, nor do I want any long commitments."

"I understand," she said, "My offer is still there."

"If you are sure this is what you want, I will be more than willing to give you as much pleasure as I can."

"That is all I want," she sighed.

Grabbing my hand, she led me to her bedroom. Watching her body movements, following her, was pure pleasure. The girl was as sexy as hell.

In her room, I stood mesmerized as I watched her begin to undress. Everything about Sally was tiny, yet she was as femininely curved as any girl he had ever been with. Everything about her was pure sex. Facing me in a bra and panties began to make her anxious.

Before she became too nervous, I quickly stripped. Everything came off before she completed her undressing. Seeing my erection, her eyes widened. When she saw what she was getting, she opened her mouth to say something, but stopped.

When she took off her bra, the sight of her perfectly shaped breasts with large, pink nipples had the best effect on me. Just looking at her had made me hard as hell. Without hesitation, she gave me a hungry smile, then pulled down her panties. The hair between her solid thighs matched the hair on her head. Her hips were rounded, while her waist looked minuscule. Lifting her arms, she did a twirl, showing me a tiny but well-shaped bottom.

"How is it some guy hasn't been smart enough to have worked at a good relationship with you?" I asked.

With a smile, she slid onto the bed. Not wanting to waste time, lest she change her mind, I slid in next to her. Taking her into my arms, I marveled at the feel of her body against mine. Feeling her tiny feminine charms pressing against me was overpowering.

I began by kissing, and she responded fully. Running my hands over her tiny body was pure pleasure. I had no idea what triggered her climax, but all of a sudden, she screamed.   Her body went rigid, then calmly relaxed.

Knowing she had just climaxed, I calmly placed myself between her beautiful legs.   Her eyes were glassy with passion.   Before continuing, I placed her legs over my shoulders.   From that angle, I was able to kiss her between her legs.   With a scream, her body stiffened again.   She emitted four separate screams as she climaxed again.

Having had several climaxes, it was time to give Sally what she wanted.   Placing myself at her entrance, I began my penetration. Another scream erupted.   Deep moans were emitted from deep in her throat.   I couldn't believe how tight she was.

That first time I penetrated her, it hurt me as if she were a virgin. Her tightness and the way her body moved, once I completed my penetration, were extraordinary.   I didn't know how long I could last.

Our first time wasn't quick, but it wasn't enough for us either.   Not long after, we were at each other again.   This time we developed a great rhythm.   After our second time, our exhaustion put us to sleep.   It was my first good night's sleep I had had in a long time.   In the morning, after one fantastic night, I told her what I thought.

"Sally, there is nothing wrong with you," I said softly, "I'm flattered you let me be with you like this.   You are a fantastic bed partner and a beautiful person inside and out."

She sighed in contentment, "After last night," she said, "you made a believer of me.   You showed me, it is the man you are with, how a woman receives her pleasure.   The man has everything to do with what gives a woman satisfaction."

"Not everything."

"What do you mean?"

"The woman has to really want the man to make him do his best for her."

"Well, I really wanted you and God, you were fantastic,"

"There is some lucky guy out there that is going to get a fantastic woman, once he finds you."

"Thanks for the beautiful one night," she said, "I will remember this night, as long as I live."

"To be honest, after last night, I am going to miss you terribly. If you ever need a man, give me a call. I'll be glad to spend another night or two with you."

THIRTY-SIX

SALLY

When Julia called me last night, I didn't know what to think. I've only dated guys my age or a year older. The gut she wanted to fix me up with was eight years older. He might feel I am much too young and immature for him.

Talking me into it, I had to admit he sounded like a perfect match, but I was still apprehensive. I have met her husband once, and to be honest, I was disappointed for her, but I would never say that to her. Why she married him, I'll never know.

When I got to her place, I was impressed. It had a pool and a hot tub. Maybe I'll change places. When I walked in, I saw her. We immediately hugged. Almost immediately, Julia and her husband brought me over to meet the guy.

"Bruce, I want you to meet my husband, Henry, and my best friend, Sally."

Standing, Bruce offered to Henry.

"Hi, Henry," Bruce said.

I couldn't believe Julia's husband ignored the hand. Being ignored must have made him angry, but he didn't show it. When he was introduced to me, I quickly took his hand. His hand felt huge in mine, yet it didn't hurt.

"Hi, Bruce," I said warmly.

"Who is this guy?" Henry asked.

"I told you, Henry. I met Bruce here yesterday, here at the pool," Julia stated, "and since Sally is single, I thought maybe the two of them would like to date."

From his face, I could tell he liked what he was seeing.

"Do you mind me asking your age?" he asked, "I want to be sure I'm not breaking any rules."

I laughed, then said, "I understand. I'm eighteen."

"Would you mind driving?" Julia asked, "My husband likes to drink."

The four of us went to a bar on the outskirts of town. Knowing I was so young, Bruce ordered soft drinks for him and I. Henry had to be the exception.

As soon as the music began, Bruce asked me to dance. Loving to dance, I was light on my feet. Bruce led us around the floor with hardly any effort. As we turned on the floor, I noticed Henry hadn't asked Julia. It was easy to see Julia disappointed when Henry wouldn't ask her to dance.

"Sally, would you mind if I asked Julia to dance?" Bruce asked.

"No. being her husband is ignoring her, I was going to suggest you do that," I told him.

After bringing me back to the table, we sat for a while and sipped our drinks. When Bruce was sure I was comfortable and the music began, he walked over to Henry.

"Would you mind if I asked your wife to dance?" Bruce asked.

Henry just sat there, ignoring Bruce.

"I'd love to dance with you," Julia cut in.

I watched them on the floor. They dance in the old-fashioned way, hardly touching. When the dance ended, Bruce brought her back to the table. I couldn't believe what happened. Julia's husband acted like a child, shouting angrily.

After his tirade, he left, leaving his wife alone. Not knowing what to say, Bruce stayed with me the rest of the night. Feeling sorry for Julia, after our last dance, I told Bruce to ask Julia again.

"Bruce, now that her husband is gone, why don't you ask Julia to dance again?"

Bruce understood what I was asking. Back at the table, he went to Julia.

"Would you like to dance one last time?" he asked her.

It was obvious Bruce had feelings for Julia. Tears were rimming her eyes. She had all she could do not to break down and cry. When Bruce got her on the floor, Julia melted into his arms, not like she did their first dance. He seemed to hold Julia closer this time. When they got back to the table, Bruce asked,

"What is going to happen when you get home?" he asked.

"I have no idea," Julia said, "I guess inviting you to be with Sally didn't sit well with Henry."

"I gathered that. Does he think there is something going on between you and me?"

"Well, he would be wrong. But in defense of you, if I were single, that would be a different story. But as it is, I am married and you are with Sally."

Leaving the establishment, he dropped Julia at her home, then drove me to me place. I didn't want this evening to end. When he stopped, I didn't get right out, but turned in my seat to face him.

"I had a wonderful time tonight, Bruce. Would you like to come up for a nightcap?" I asked.

"Sure."

After parking, to show me what a gentleman he was, he took my hand and walked me to my apartment.

"You're a great guy, Bruce," I told him, "I had a great time."

"You are a great gal too, Sally," he said, "You know how to treat a guy."

"How did I give you such a nice time?" I asked.

"Just being you was nice."

"I'll take that as a compliment."

"It was meant to be," he said.

Once inside my apartment, I should have felt terrible about lying to him, but I didn't.

"Actually, I lied," I told him, "I didn't have anything to drink. I asked you to come in so I can spend more time with you."

"I really didn't need anything to drink anyway," he said.

"Do you and Julia have anything going?" I asked suddenly.

"No, Julia and I are just friends. Why do you ask?"

"I asked because, if you two had something going, I wouldn't want to interfere."

"Why would you think we had something going?"

"I can see how the two of you act around each other."

"To be honest, I wasn't aware of doing anything special," he said.

"Then I'm going to be honest with you," I said shyly, "Being with you makes me want more. Being in your arms got me wildly turned on.

"Sally I."

"Let me finish," I said, holding up a hand, "I've had sex just one time in my life. It wasn't very satisfying. Now, I need to know, no, I want to know my true feelings about sex."

"Are you're asking me to spend the night?"

"Yes," she said, "I need desperately to know what real sex is like."

"Sally, you're a beautiful woman and could have your pick of any guy you want."

"The only boys I know are my age, or a year older. None of them fit the image I want. Now, I know you are a few years older than me, but your experience is what I want and need."

"Are you sure this is what you want to do?"

"Just saying those words to you has cost me a lot. Just to get up the nerve to tell you how I feel, makes me feel..."

"Whatever you feel would be wrong. I am flattered you have asked. Now, I want to know if you are really sure you want to do this? I would be honored to spend the night with you. But I have to be honest with you. I'm not in the market for a wife, nor do I want any long commitments."

"I understand," she said, "My offer is still there."

"If you are sure this is what you want, I will be more than willing to give you as much pleasure as I can."

"That is all I want," I sighed.

Grabbing his hand, I led him to my bedroom. In my room, he watched me undress. Then he quickly stripped. He was naked before I finished undressing.

When I saw his erection, I couldn't believe my eyes. What he had for me scared me. Then, before he changed his mind, I took off my bra. He liked what he was seeing. Feeling good, I gave him a hungry smile, then pulled down my panties. Knowing he liked what he saw, lifted my arms and did a twirl, showing him my naked body.

"How is it some guy hasn't been smart enough to have worked at a good relationship with you?" he asked.

With a smile, I slid into the bed. He slid in next to me, taking me into my arms. As he kissed me, I couldn't help but respond. As he moved his hands over my body, I felt nothing but pleasure. Suddenly, something inside me made me scream. My body went rigid, then calmly relaxed.

Knowing I had just climaxed, I calmly waited as he placed himself between my legs. Continuing, he placed my legs over his shoulders. Then he did what I never expected: he kissed me between my legs. I screamed again as he sent me into oblivion.

Having had several climaxes, he finally gave me what I wanted. He placed himself at my entrance and began his penetration. He was driving me crazy as another scream erupted from me. He felt as if he were stretching me. Our first time was quick.

It wasn't enough for me, I needed more. Then we were at each other again. This time, he developed a great rhythm. After our second time, our exhaustion put us to sleep.

"After last night," she said, "you made a believer of me.

"There is some lucky guy out there that is going to get a fantastic woman, once he finds you."

"Thanks for the beautiful one night," she said, "I will remember this night, as long as I live."

THIRTY-SEVEN

BRUCE

After spending the night with Sally, I left her place with mixed feelings. I could get to liking her, even if she was so much younger. In a few years, our age difference wouldn't make any difference.

What I felt for Julia was something I shouldn't be feeling. It was a weird feeling. Since I had never had sex with Julia, those feelings shouldn't be there.

The next day, I didn't see Julia at all. The few times we did meet at the pool weren't as bad as I thought. We sort of stayed away from each other. Whenever we did see each other, we would nod in recognition, but we went our separate ways.

Almost like clockwork, whenever Julia and I were at the apartment swimming, not together, or in the hot tub, Henry would materialize a few minutes later. He just had to see what would Julia was doing. It was evident to me, Henry thinks there is something going on between me and Julia.

As much as I would love to bed Julia, that could never happen under these circumstances. I had too much respect for Julia to try and attempt to get her into my bed. Anyway, she had made it clear, she wanted only to be friends.

One Saturday afternoon, while I was alone in the Jacuzzi, suddenly Julia appeared. Without hesitation, she slid in next to me. I thought about moving, but it was obvious she wanted to talk.

"Where is Henry?" I asked.

"He is on duty today."

"How are things going between the two of you?"

"Things could be better, but he still doesn't trust me."

"There is no reason for him not to trust you. You haven't done anything wrong. Holding a grudge on something is stupid. Grudges for this long is unhealthy."

"That is just the way he is," Julia said.

"How can you live with a guy who doesn't trust you?"

"It isn't easy, believe me, but he is my husband."

"His attitude is another reason why I never wanted to get involved with a married woman. The thought of that happening to me scares the hell out me. Myself, I would never put up with that kind of attitude."

"So, you don't trust either."

"I do trust," I said, "but I depends upon the situation and the person. Maybe that is why I am like I am."

"It's too bad. Your one hell of a nice guy."

"Don't get me wrong. I love women and I treat them with total respect, but..."

"You don't have to go into detail," she said, "I understand."

Spending the day together, without Henry popping in, was a great treat for me. For some reason, Julia always enjoyed my company. Henry doesn't know how lucky he is to have Julia. Most men would die for a woman like her.

For the next two weeks, while Henry was free to spy on his wife, everyone was back to playing the same game. Julia and I acknowledged each other but with slight glances and winks. Other than that, we didn't talk. Then one day, Julia surprisingly came to the hot tub crying. Seeing her crying, I wondered where Henry was. I had to be sure Henry wasn't around.

"What's up, Julia?"

"Henry got his orders."

"Where is he going?"

"He's staying here, but going to a battalion."

"What are you going to do?"

"He wants me to go home until he gets back."

"What do you want?"

"I'd like to stay here. I hate a lot of traveling, and I don't get along with my mother very well, especially since she got married again."

"Then stay here. Once he is gone, there isn't anything he can do about it."

"That will only cause more friction."

"Well, the decision is yours. You will have to make up your own mind what you want to do and stick to it."

Sitting quietly in the Jacuzzi, soaking, Julia suddenly became quiet, as if she was thinking about what I had told her. Enjoying the serenity and each other's company, we laid our heads back on the edge of the tub and closed our eyes. As close as we were sitting, our hands accidentally touched.

THIRTY-EIGHT

BRUCE

The touch was as if a charge of electricity had been turned on. Turning our heads, we looked at each other, stunned. Since neither of us moved our hands away, we clasped fingers. Immediately, my heart rate doubled, and I became hard.

"Since I have met you," Julia said, "My life has been in turmoil."

"Why is that?"

"Seeing the way you act around different people makes me wish Henry was that kind of man."

Immediately changing the subject, I brought Henry into the conversation.

"When does Henry leave?"

"I guess he goes to training in two weeks."

"Well, if you ever get in a situation or need company some reason, you know where to find me."

"Good, because I'm going to need your strength," she said.

At that moment, another couple came around the wall. Immediately, we dropped hands. Guilty feelings caught us. I wanted to leave the hot tub, but couldn't for a while. When my hardness relaxed, I went to the main pool for a swim.

"That was close," Julia said.

"You don't know how close."

"No, I don't, but I like being with you. You make me feel like a woman."

"I'm happy I make you feel that way."

It wasn't long before Julia told me, Henry was due home from work. It was time for Julia to go back to her apartment. Loneliness set in the minute Julia left. With what I was doing, I knew I would be asking for trouble, but Julia did something to me.

THIRTY-NINE

JULIA

The day Henry was to leave for training, I went to the airport with him. Henry seemed distant to me. When he hugged and kissed me, his kiss didn't seem to have the old intensity. His kiss was as if he were in a hurry to get away.

Once Henry boarded the plane, because of his lack of passion, I began to feel lost and lonely. Standing at the window, watching the plane disappear in the distance, my loneliness became unbearable; it was the first time I was alone and scared.

Feeling forlorn, I went back to my apartment with an incentive to do nothing but exist. In a daze, I turned on the television. Knowing Bruce was at work, I couldn't concentrate on any program. Then, strangely enough, as I was sitting there, staring into space, I realized I wasn't missing Henry, I was actually missing Bruce. What was it about Bruce that seemed to turn my world upside down?

Two days later, the moment Bruce entered the complex, I began to feel much better. Just knowing he was there, even if I couldn't be him, I began to feel wild. Without a second thought, forgetting about Henry, I changed into my sexy swimsuit, one I had never worn it in public before. Now I was ready to join Bruce in the hot tub.

Knowing Bruce had a habit of climbing into the Jacuzzi to relax, I was ready to join him. Another habit Bruce has is, when he was ready, I know he will ask me to go somewhere to dinner. With Henry not around to mess things up, I knew I had a yearning to be with Bruce. I just knew Bruce would ask me to join him.

During these last two days, there had been many times when I wished Bruce would ask me to join him. But then, knowing him as I do, I knew he would never ask, because I am married and we never knew when Henry would be around. Not knowing right from wrong, I knew I shouldn't be thinking of going anywhere with Bruce, even if he asked.

Standing in my window, waiting for Bruce to head to the Jacuzzi, I began to feel anxious. Normally, I would wait a few minutes before joining him, so he wouldn't think I was looking for him. At this moment, as Bruce disappeared around the wall, I knew I couldn't wait any longer.

Leaving my apartment, I quickly made my way to the hot tub. As quickly as I could, without seeming too obvious, I slithered into the hot tub and sat beside him.

"Oh, I didn't know you were here," I lied.

"Do you want me to leave?" he asked.

"No, as a matter of fact, I wanted to talk with you."

"Fire away," he said.

"Don't you ever cook?"

"Not for myself, I don't."

"You eat out all the time?"

"It is almost as cheap to eat out then it is to buy the food, store it, waste time cooking, and then doing the cleanup. Eating out, I get served and don't have to clean my mess."

Typical male, I thought. Then, laughing, I swallowed my fear to do something I normally wouldn't have the guts to do.

"Come to my place tonight," I uttered, "I want to make you dinner."

"Now that is an invitation I can't turn down. With Henry gone, I don't have to worry about being in the way."

After making my invitation to Bruce, I felt a slight bit of panic. What was I thinking? This isn't me. What might Bruce think? It was almost an invitation for more than food. Then quickly I thought, God, my mind is in the gutter. Between being ignored by Henry and wondering what it would be like to be with Bruce, I knew I was beginning to think like a slut. Maybe I want to act like a slut, she thought. My body and mind want it.

If Henry was here, would I be thinking like this? If Henry did his job. . . I didn't know. What I did know, Bruce turned me on, he makes me think like I never thought before. What will I do if Bruce takes advantage of the situation? He hasn't yet, but what makes me think he wouldn't now with Henry gone? Was this wishful thinking? Did I really want to know the difference between the two men?

This was crazy, thinking about sex. I have never thought about having sex with another man before. Now, all my thoughts were always about Bruce. Would sex be different with him? Then I thought, Bruce has never hinted about having sex with me. Maybe he wouldn't want to have sex with me. I know he has had sex with Sally. Sally says he is fantastic. At his age, he has probably had sex with a lot of women.

What would be the harm in being another notch in his belt? No one would ever need to know, and I would have my answer. I'd have someone to compare with. Now all I have to do is wait to see if he comes on to me. If he doesn't, do I go after him?

FORTY

BRUCE

In my mind, I know I shouldn't ever think about going to Julia's place. My feelings for her were growing too rapidly, and she is married. Eating with her, at her apartment, could be dangerous. On the other hand, if I asked her to join me at a nice public restaurant, the temptation would be gone, and it would be a lot safer for her.

It was close to five o'clock when I climbed the stairs to Julia's apartment. It only took a few seconds, after I knocked, for her to open the door. Seeing her only made my heart pump wildly. Looking at her, standing before me in light blue shorts and a matching T-shirt, was breathtaking. There didn't seem to be enough material to hide her curves. The sight stopped me cold.

"Well, come in," she said, stepping aside.

I knew this was a mistake. The moment I passed her and got a good whiff of her perfume, it almost made me forget who I am. Between the sight of her and the smell she emitted, I knew I was in trouble. In that moment, I wanted to grab her and give her a taste of what I was feeling.

"Instead of you cooking for me, let me take you out," I said quickly.

For a short moment, she almost agreed. She was deliberating. From her look, I knew there was some heavy thinking going on. What would be her reason not to accept my offer over hers? To tell the truth, because I didn't really want to take her out, I didn't push the issue.   I was willing to let happen, whatever happens.

Actually, I was really hoping that whatever was meant to happen, did happen.

She knew the situation she was putting herself in by cooking for me. Temptation would be heavy.   This was her chance to stay faithful to Henry.   This was her chance to push all those thoughts to the rear and forget them.

"No, I insist," she said nervously, "For everything you have done for me, tonight I want to make you happy."

If Julia ever knew what I wanted, to make myself happy, she would probably change her mind about having dinner here.   Smiling, I handed her a bottle of wine, which she took.   Her delicious body beckoned as she waved me to a seat.

"Take a seat and watch the ball game," she said.

"You don't have to watch ball for me," I told her.

"I'm not.   I love baseball.   Henry didn't care for sports."

Not curious, what Henry liked or didn't like, I let the subject go.

"Something smells good," I said.

"Charcoal steak and baked potatoes."

As good as the food smelled, I know it would taste even better.

"Sounds delicious,"

"How is it you always know what to say to make a girl happy?"

"If it works on you, I'll keep doing it."

Then she changed the subject.

"Have you ever seen Sally since that night?"

"Not really. We wave when we see each other, but that is the extent of our relationship."

"Did you sleep with her?"

"What?"

Julia laughed.

"When I got home, things were tense around here. For some reason, I was feeling jealousy. Did you sleep with her?"

"Would it make a difference if I did?"

"No, I'm just curious."

"They say curiosity killed the cat."
Julia turned away from me. Going back to the job at hand, she dove in. When everything was ready, Julia took the seat directly across from me. As expected, the food was as delicious as it smelled.

"You are one hell of a cook," I told her, "I'd let you cook for me anytime."

"I will if you are available," she said.

"I could make myself available," I told her, "But that will depend on you."

"Look, I would love to have sex with you, Bruce, but I am married and I'm scared as hell to do something I have never done before. Henry is the only man I have ever had sex with."

"You don't have to worry about me, Julia. As much as I'd love to be your lover, I would never do anything without you initiating it."

"Well, I guess that is laying it on the line," she said, "If I do come to you, it won't be for a while. But you can bet, if I ever do cheat on Henry, it will be with you."

"Don't worry. I will never pressure you into anything. All I ask is to let me treat you to dinner now and then."

With a smile, she began clearing the table.

"You start the dishes," I told her, "I finish clearing the table and dry the dishes."

"You don't have to do that, it's a woman's job."

"And I suppose it is the woman 's job to do all the cooking, too."

"Yes.

"Who says?"

"Henry."

"Doesn't he ever help you?"

"Never."

"Then, since you did the cooking, I want you to sit down to

watch the ball game while I do the dishes."

"Oh no," she said, putting up her hands, "I wouldn't feel right doing that. But I will let you help me, so we can watch the game together."

"Okay, I won't argue that point with you."

Standing side by side, we did the dishes. After everything was done, we went to the living room. The game was in the seventh inning.

"Shit," she cried, "I'm losing."

"Oh, that is too bad," I teased, "My team is winning."

"Are we going to clash like this all the time?"

"Only in fun," I answered, "You're much to pretty for me to take the chance on losing your friendship."

"Bruce, there is no way you will ever drive me away from you. The question is going to be, how close do I want to keep you."

"Let me put it this way. I'll stay at arm's length, as long as you want me to. If I ever get the chance to sample your delectable body, it will be all the much sweeter."

"You know how to make a girl melt."

When the game was over, I didn't want to cause any problems, so I got up and left.

"I think it best if I go to my own place," I told her. "Thank you for such an unforgettable evening. Next time, if you are in a mind to let me, it is my turn to treat you."

"All you have to do is ask," she said.

"You have an open invitation. It is up to you if you want to use the invitation."

Julia followed me to the door. Opening the door, I turned to face her one last time. My lips burned with the need to kiss her, but that would not be fair. If we ever did kiss, it had to be her doing. Stepping outside, I turned to face one of the last times. Julia stood in the doorway watching me walk away.

Forty-One

Julia

Watching Bruce walk away was very difficult for me. After closing the door, I leaned against it. After closing the door, I began thinking about the opportunity I had just let slip through my fingers. There was a longing that was driving me wild with need, and I knew I blew it. All I had to do was touch him and plead with my eyes. It is a shame Bruce is a gentleman. No other guy would have walked away. Any other guy would have been all over me in a heartbeat.

The one night was the breaking point. I went through a lot of trouble to get Sally to meet Bruce. When the four of us were together, it turned out to be a big mistake. Since then, everything about my life seemed to have changed for me. That was three weeks ago.

Since that night, Henry has never tried to have sex with me, not even once. Now, after one night of just dinner with Bruce, my passion for sex has risen to new heights.

Walking away from the door, I felt stupid. As I turned off all the lights and made sure the windows and doors were locked, I went to bed in a bad mood. In a fury with myself for batching, I undressed, leaving my clothes where they fell.

Going into the bathroom, I gazed at my body in the mirror. I was proud of what I saw. My legs were still long and nicely shaped. Then I marveled at my flat tummy with shapely hips. With no children, my hips were slender, but had a nice curve to them. My large breasts looked a little heavy, but still had a nice shape. Now my pink nipples had hardened at the thought of what I let escape me.

Feeling somewhat lost, from my own error, I saw frustration with tears forming in my eyes. Damn, I was feeling so aroused, and I could have fixed that tonight. What is Henry's problem? He had always been after me before we got married. There were times when I didn't want sex, but gave in to him anyway.

Tonight was the first time I had felt such a need in a long time. Tonight, I really wanted sex, but my need wasn't centered on my husband, Henry. What should I do? How would I feel if I let my need take over?

I have even gone to dinner with Bruce twice after that night, plus he came here, to my place, a couple of times. Every time I had Bruce here, at my place, no matter how much I wanted him, I found I didn't have the guts to seduce him. Was I turning into a wanton woman? God, lately my need for sex was nearly overpowering.

The day Henry came home, I was at the airport to welcome him home. Opening my arms to him, he came to me willingly, but when he kissed me, it was hardly with any passion. There was definitely something wrong. Henry's attitude was making me think he didn't care anymore.

The entire time of his stay-at-home, Henry hardly ever spoke to me. To my surprise, Henry made love to me, one unsatisfying time, before he left.

"Okay, Henry, what is going on?"

"Did you fuck him while I was gone?"

"Jesus Christ," I swore, "what kind of a woman do you think I am?"

"After that one night, I am beginning to wonder."

"Are you referring to that night the four of us went out?"

"Yes. He played you like a fiddle and you enjoyed it."

"Any woman would like that kind of attention, but that doesn't mean anything was going to happen between us."

Ignoring my tirade, Henry walked away. Slamming the door, he got into his car and drove away. A few hours later, when Henry came home, he was drunk. The moment Henry came home, he went to bed. Angry and hurt, I slept on the couch.

The next morning, we ate breakfast in silence. When Henry left for work, I broke down and cried. What was happening to our marriage? How could Henry think I was being unfaithful to him? I had to admit, recently I had thought about cheating, but knew I didn't have the guts.

Three weeks later, as Henry was getting ready for deployment, I confronted him.

"During these three weeks, while have been home, you have only made love to me one time, and that one time was not satisfying."

Henry, being Henry, he never said a word.

"Henry, don't you love me anymore?"

"Yes, I love you," he stated, "I have always loved you, but I can't handle this situation with Bruce."

"There is nothing between Bruce and me, except friendship, and there never will be anything else."

He listened, then hesitated before saying what he was thinking.

"Look, Julia," he said harshly, "my enlistment will be over when I get back from deployment. I will be taking my discharge and going back home. That is when I will know your true feelings. If you go home with me, I will know I am your man, if not? So be it."

Torn by his words, I didn't know what to do or say. Henry had laid it on the line. What were my true feelings? My guess, only time will tell. Going with Henry to the airport the next day, I kissed him goodbye. Sadly, I didn't feel anything besides numbness.

In bed that night, I cried myself to sleep. My mind was in turmoil. What hurt was my body, trying to betray me.   Damn you, Henry, why couldn't he have been more attentive to me?   It has been almost two months, and we have had sex two times.   It wasn't making love, as I expected it to be.   My need for love and attention was definitely driving me crazy.

My need for attention was growing so quickly, I didn't know how I would handle it when Bruce was around.   God, it would be another nine months before I saw him again.   Could I stay faithful in all that time? Nine months is a long time to go without sex.

I thought about getting a job to pass the time and meet new friends. Trying to avoid Bruce, Sally and I went out to dinner a few times.   It was weird since all Sally could talk about was Bruce.   The girl was in love with him, knowing she could never have him the way she wanted, she wasn't going to chase him.

Maybe that is what I should do.   The only problem is, I see him all the time.   Maybe I should pack and go home until Henry comes back, but then, I don't think I could handle being around my mother's new husband.

Being I have only seen Bruce at the pool was a help, but seeing him only made me want him.   Maybe I should just let nature take its course. What will happen will happen.   My fighting the situation was only causing me heartache.

FORTY-TWO

BRUCE

Damn, that woman has left me hanging. What I wouldn't do for that woman. But then, I had to remember, Henry would be home in a couple of weeks. To be fair to her, by doing something stupid, I would be ruining a good relationship.

In my own bed, I had trouble getting to sleep. My body and mind were restless with need and desire. That woman has a deep hold on me. Unable to sleep, I turned on the light. Picking up my book, I began to read. Eventually my eyes grew tire, then closing them, I drifted off to sleep.

Unable to stop thinking about Julia, I found it didn't help to go against my vow and not to call her. I needed to hear her voice.

"Hello," she said.

"You sound down in the dumps. Are you hungry?"

"Bruce, I'm so glad you called."

"I wasn't going to, but knowing Henry was gone, I thought you might need some cheering up."

"To be honest, I don't feel like going anywhere tonight."

"Here is one last try," I said, desperately, "How about a couple drinks and some dancing?"

There was some hesitation. For a while, I thought I had screwed up. Not hearing a sound, I was about to hang up when she spoke.

"Oh, hell, let's get drunk," she uttered.

"Do you want to come down or do you want to come up to get you?"

"I'll be down in five minutes," she said.

One minute later, someone knocked on my door. Hearing the knock, I wondered who was here. Opening the door, I was surprised to see Julia standing there.

"You must be in a hurry," I said, "Your early."

"Yes, I am. I need to blow off some steam."

"Please don't do that," I chuckled.

She began to laugh with me.

"To be honest, I just wanted to be funny. I had no idea what I was saying," she said, blushing.

With a smile of satisfaction, I grabbed her hand, not thinking. Holding onto it tightly, I led her to the parking lot. Ready for a night out, Julia moved with me at my speed. Again, I was to be the gentleman. Going to and from, I helped her in and out of the car. I wanted to be sure she was comfortable and buckled up each time.

Julia was having so much fun, being waited on and being paid attention to, she didn't care who saw her out on the town. Slipping an arm around my waist, she snuggled up to me. Reciprocating, I slid an arm over her shoulders.

"Your touch feels so good," she cooed, snuggling tighter.

"You feel good to me, too," I whispered.

Inside, we found the lights were down low. Though the room was dark, we made our way to one of the free tables. No sooner had we sat down than the waitress was at our table.

After taking our order, the waitress disappeared. Instead of waiting for the waitress to return with our drinks, I led Julia to the floor. My need to hold her in my arms was my biggest priority.

As soon as I took her into my arms, she wound her arms tightly around my neck. Adding fuel to the fire, she snuggled as close to me as she could get. Feeling her closeness and enjoying it, the waitress would have to wait to be paid for the drinks.

"I'm glad I came," Julia cooed.

Holding her tightly, we moved in perfect rhythm around the floor. The feel of her fantastic body pressing against me, along with the smell of her perfume, was setting me on fire. Being Julia was so tall, only a few inches shorter than me, I found her neck accessible. Even though I promised not to push, seeing her neck so free, I couldn't resist. Brushing her hair aside, I kissed her neck.

"Ooooh," she moaned.

As she moaned, she pushed her hips into mine. She had to feel my erection. Feeling her body pressing so close against mine made my senses soar. I could resist kissing her neck a second time.

"You had better be careful," she whispered.

"I'm always careful."

"I think, maybe we should sit for a while," she said.

It was obvious to me, her breath had become ragged.

"I think I need my drink," she said.

I kept my arm around her waist as I led her back to the table. There I found the waitress waiting. First, I made sure Julia was comfortable, then I paid the waitress with a nice tip for being patient.

"Thanks," she murmured.

"It was all my pleasure."

Sitting back in the chair, Julia stared into my eyes. Her stare made my heart beat wildly. Returning her stare, I blew her a kiss.

"What was that for?"

"Because I have been wanting to kiss you since I first met you," I told her, "And because I promised not to push you, I decided to blow you a kiss instead."

"Why don't you try kissing me the way a man does, to find out how I will react?"

Getting out of my seat, I circled behind her. Unexpectedly, Julia stood and turned to face me. Before I could put my arms around her, she threw her arms around my neck. As my hands landed on her hips, she pursed her lips for a kiss. At that moment, I didn't care where we were or who saw us. I wasn't going to lose this opportunity. Grabbing her around the waist, I pulled her close. Leaning back, she pushed her hips into me again and smiled.

"Get a room," someone shouted.

People laughed and clapped.

"Here is the kiss you want," she said.

Her soft, wet lips pressed against mine, making me caught my breath. As the kiss began, her legs suddenly became weak. Tightening my hold on her, so she wouldn't fall, I led her onto the floor.

"Let's dance," I said.

On the floor, as she melted into my arms. Plastered against each other, she offered her lips again. Her heart was beating as wildly as mine. Pressing our lips together, we actually stopped dancing. As tempted as I was, I didn't let my hand drop below her lower back. Our kiss lasted longer than anyone expected.

"My God," Julia gasped.

Shouts and whistles could be heard around the room.

Laying her head on my shoulder, we began moving. Not to the music but to the beat of our own. In another world, we bumped into other dancers. Being in the middle of a group, I finally let my hand drop to cup her curvy bottom. Her eyes widened, but she didn't stop me. Instead, a low moan escaped her lips.

"Have you had enough to drink?" I asked.

"No," she gasped, "I think I'm going to need a little more to loosen up for what's to come."

"And what would that be?" I asked.

She was laughing as I led her back to our table. To give her time to come down, I ordered another round. Sitting at the table, we reached across it to hold hands. Neither of us could take our eyes off the other.

"I'm scare, Bruce."

"We don't have to do anything."

"But I want to," she cried, "I need to."

"Are you sure you are ready?"

"Yes and no."

I waited for her to continue. As much as I wanted and needed her, I was determined to stick to my rule. Julia would have to be the person to make the first move.

"I do want you, but I also feel guilty for feeling this way."

"As I said, we don't have to do anything," I whispered, "Just being with you like this, holding you like this, will have to be enough for now."

"But I want to know how it feels to be in another man's arms. A man who totally wants me."

"Well, you have the man who really wants you. But you really have to want me to. It isn't any good if you use me, just see what sex with a different man is like. I want you to want me. You have to want me and have genuine feeling for me."

"The truth. I have deep feelings for you. Real deep, but you have said, you don't want marriage or long relationships."

"Yes, I have said that, but…You are making me see differently."
"That is another problem. I am married. I might not love him as I used to, but he is my husband."

"As I said before, and I will say it again. I want you very badly, but if you do not want me the same way, because you are married, then it wouldn't be good."

"As you said, you want me because you have deep feelings for me, then I want you for the same reason. Although there isn't much we can do about it, I think I am in love with you."

"And I with you, but you are married, so I can't have you."

"You can have me, so what do we do now?"

FORTY-THREE

JULIA

"You have danced with other men, haven't you?" he asked

"Yes, but I have never had these feeling with any of them," I said, "You are the first to make me think outside my comfort zone."

"I did notice, you didn't take long to get me in the mood."

"I can tell, too."

Standing, Bruce pulled me from the chair. As I came to my feet, I let him slide his arm around my waist. When he pulled me tightly against his hard body, I wiggled my hips as he led me to the floor.

"Tease," he said.

"You are the tease," I responded, "Your magic wand puts me in a mood, I shouldn't be in."

Dancing our last dance, we found we couldn't control our passion. Our passion was growing leaps and bounds. As our passion went beyond temptation, we decided to leave. On our way out, we stopped at the table, but never finished our last drink. Leaving in a hurry, we made it out the door clinging together.

With temptation so great, we stopped just outside the door. Wrapping our arms around each other, we kissed deeply. The ride home was silent.   I tried staring out the side window while Bruce tried concentrating on the road.   Getting back to the apartment building, Bruce made a hasty stop. Turning off the engine, we were at each other again.

"God, I can't take much more of this," I groaned.

"You do have a way of making me push temptation aside," Bruce whispered.

Getting out of the car, we hurried hand in hand to my apartment. At the door, Bruce took my keys to open the door.   By that time, I was so aroused, once he had the door open, I wound my arms around his neck.   I didn't care who saw us.   To get my way, I teased him with my tongue.   When I broke the kiss, I asked.

 "Are you coming in?"

"Not tonight, Julia," I think you need more time."

"What makes you think that?"

"I just do.   Let's wait a day or two."

"I don't want to wait any longer," I told him.

"You need time to think this through," he said, "You have never had an affair before, and I want you to be sure this is really what you want. If we do tonight, what we both desperately to do, you might regret what it in the morning.   I don't want you to have any regrets.   You have to be one hundred percent sure this is what you really want, before we take this to the next level."

His refusal really upset me.   He wants me, I know he does.   Feeling his erection pressing into me when we kiss makes me wonder why is he turning me down?   Is it because of Henry?   Well, this isn't over.   He will be in my bed before this is over.

In bed, I cried like a baby.   First, her husband doesn't want me, now the guy I thought would make love to me was also making me wait.   The next day, I made sure that when Bruce came through the gate, I would be sitting on a lounge, wearing my sexy yellow bikini.   Stopping before me, he stared down into my eyes.   He was wondering if I was going to tell him off for last night.

"Bruce, I did a lot of thinking last night."

It was my turn to tease him.

"And?" he said, staring at me.

"And I'd like to try last night all over again," I told him, "This time the bar bill will be on me.   If you turned me down again, I will assume you don't want to be with me."

"If you feel that sure about how you feel, we don't have to go out," he said, "I'll order takeout.   That way, we can begin enjoying each other right away."

"We could do that, but no.   I loved the way you made me feel last night.   My only question is, was it just the thrill of our time together, or was what we were feeling the real thing?"

"For me, it was the real thing, but if you insist, where and when would you like to go?" he asked.

"Come with me," I told him.

In the car, I drove in a different direction.   I didn't want him to know where we were going.   Stopping at a little bar, where a band was playing country western music, we went inside.   Bruce got us a table and then ordered drinks.   Taking me onto the dance floor, I couldn't help but to melt into his arms.   Holding him so tightly, I could feel his excitement through his jeans.

"Damn, your hot," he told me.

"Yes, but I want you hotter," I told him.

"If you get me much hotter, I might not make it through the night," he teased.

I laughed and said, "I wanted to make you beg, but the joke is on me. I can't wait to get you into bed."

When we got back to the apartment, we were in a hurry. Entering the apartment, I didn't want to wait any longer.

"Let's have some good homemade exercise before we head to the hot tub," I said. "Afterward, we can rush back to finish the night with more exciting exercise, before we sleep."

"That sounds like a perfect plan."

We undressed as if our clothes were on fire. This was going to be the first time Bruce saw me naked. He knows what I look like in a bikini, but now I get to see him completely naked.

After dropping my clothes, except her bra and panties, I didn't want to finish until he was stark naked. Seeing him naked and erect, his size sort of scared me.

"Jesus," I cried, "Will that fit?"

"Of course, it will fit."

I wasn't too sure, but now seeing what he was offering made me want him even more.

"Be gentle with me," I told him.

I didn't know if I could easily take his size, but seeing what he had, I was sure as hell I wanted to find out.

Climbing on the bed, I quickly laid back in the bed. Seeing him standing there ready, I not only opened my arms but my legs too. With a huge smile on my face, I began licking my lips to entice him.

"If you want some enjoyment," I told him, come and get it."

He quickly slid onto the bed with me. As he took her into his arms, he felt so different from Henry. Bruce was bigger all over. He made me feel protected and warm. His kisses burn with white hot passion.

When Bruce finally moved between my open thighs and slid his hands beneath me, to grasp my butt, he lifted me from the mattress. When he placed my legs over his shoulders, I began to wonder what he was doing. My husband never did anything like this.

Then his lips a tongue touched my vagina. Never had I ever felt such pleasure; I went ballistic.

"Jesus H Christ," I screamed.

My body completely betrayed me. He touched my most sensitive parts with his tongue. Unable to control myself, I began bucking and shaking with uncontrollable emotions. Closing my eyes, my head rolled on the pillow as I groaned.

"You bastard," I moaned, "Please stop teasing me."

Laughing, he put me back to the mattress, where he began working his erection back and forth across the lips of my vagina. Every time he paused at my entrance, I moaned. Raising my hips to capture him didn't help.

"God damn you," I moaned.

When he finally had enough, I felt him enter inside me. He took me slowly, painfully slow. The feel of him stretching me was enough to make me groan with pleasure. With more length entering, I screamed a few more times.

I was blown away. I never dreamed sex could be so good. When he was most of the way in, he finally, with trust, gave me every inch. Not wanting him to get away, I encircled his body with my arms and legs. All of a sudden, I couldn't help myself, I began thrusting my hips to match his thrusts. My movements caused him a quick release. As he rolled from me, I felt blown away.

"Holly shit," I cried, "I have never been fucked like that before."

"And we are not done yet," he told me, "But first we need some fuel."

Bruce ordered Pizza.   After two pieces, I couldn't wait for more loving. I didn't have to pull him very hard.   In bed, I pushed him to his back.   As he lay there watching me, I moved him.   Having never done this before, it was like it was natural.

Lifting my hips, I put him at my wet opening.   This time, he penetration was easier.   Sinking down on his erection, I began riding him as if I were riding a horse.   I had never felt anything like this in my life. With the intensity of our climax, we quickly dropped off to sleep.

FORTY-FOUR

BRUCE

Early the next morning, I got up early. Not wanting to see Julia until later tonight, I left for work early. In my mind, she needed extra time to be sure she wasn't making a mistake.

Having a difficult time keeping my mind on my work, the people I worked with sensed something was bothering me. When Jeff cornered me, he made sure the guards stayed on extra vigil, while we talked. No one except Jeff would dare bring up any subject when I was in this mood. Everyone else was willing to let me work off my problems on my own.

At the end of my work day, not knowing if I was doing the right thing or not, I took my time going home. In one way, I was dying to see Julia, but on the other hand, because of the circumstances, I knew what I wanted was wrong. How was I going to feel if Julia told me I was right and she didn't want me after all?

Then, thinking about last night, I knew I could have had her, but I didn't want to take her the way things were. Was that a mistake? If I had taken what was offered, I could have damaged our relationship. Then again. Why would I have cared if our relationship was damaged? She's married, and there are other women available. With another woman, I wouldn't have to be so careful.

Turning down a woman who is so desirable didn't make me feel very smart. Doing the right thing isn't always the right thing. I might have talked myself out of an enjoyable night in heaven, with a very beautiful woman I care for.

As I came through the gate, I saw Julia sitting on a lounge by the pool as if she were waiting for me.   This was the part I was going to hate.   The look on her face didn't look to promising.   Stopping, I looked into her eyes.   Expecting Julia to turn me down, I felt terrible.

"Bruce, as you said last night, I did a lot of thinking."

"And?" I said, staring at her.

"And I'd like to try last night all over again," she said, "This time the bar bill will be on me.   If you turned me down again, I will have to assume you don't want to be with me.""

"If you feel that sure about how you feel, we don't have to go out. I'll order takeout, and we can begin enjoying each other early."

"We could do that, but no.   I loved the way you made me feel last night.   Was it just the thrill, or were the feelings we were feeling real?"

"For me, they were real, but I was afraid you hate me after for taking advantage of you," I said, "Now that is clear, when and where would you like to go?"

"How about we go right now," she said, smiling, "We can order a sandwich, along with drinks, and dance a few dances to the Jukebox. After our first dance, I will know how I really feel.   Last night, when you turned me down, you made me think I was wrong for feeling how I felt."

"You weren't wrong.   You were just undecided.   If we would have gone through with what we both wanted, I wasn't sure how you would feel about me the next morning."

"I understand your feelings," she said, "That is why I need to be sure. I am sure, by taking you out tonight, I will find out."

"I won't do anything tonight, except to make love to you.   I don't want to just fuck you.   I want to make love with you.   Last night, I wanted you so badly, I hardly sleep. I just didn't want you losing respect for yourself."

"Shut up," she chuckled, "Get ready for a wonderful night."

"Just going out with you makes it wonderful for me," I told her.

"Get into my car," she ordered, "I'm also driving tonight."

"Are you always this bossy?" I chuckled.

"Only when I want something," she said, glaring at me. From the look she gave me, I knew it was time to keep my big mouth shut.

"In that case, lead on, sweet lady."

Getting in her car, I purposely stayed away from her. When I didn't attempt to move closer to her, she gave me a sharp look. Then, to my surprise, Julia drove off in a different direction. Not saying anything, I waited to see where she was taking me.

Julia stopped at a bar I had never been to before. Before going inside, we sat and listened to a band playing country western music.

"Does the music sound good to you?" she asked.

"As long as we are together, any music will do," I said.

Laughing, we got out of the car. Inside, I found a table, ordered drinks, and began dancing. After that first dance, it became obvious to me, Julia knew she was going to get what she wanted. The way she held on to me and sighed, there was no doubt what she wanted. Now, I was wondering what Julia was feeling. Did she want to tease, or forget about dancing and go home early? The night was young. If she wanted to go home now, we would have more time for sex.

"Damn, your hot," I told her.

"Yes, but I want you hotter."

"If you make me much hotter, I might not make it through the night," I teased.

"If you disappoint me tonight, I will have to kill you."

"Oh, I have no intention of disappointing you tonight or any other night. If we left right now, it wouldn't be soon enough."

Laughing, she said, "I wanted to make you beg for it like you did me, but the joke is on me. I can't wait any longer to get you into bed."

By saying what I did, it was enough to make her break our dance. There wasn't any shame as she stopped, took my hand, and left the floor in the middle of the dance. We didn't even stop to finish their drinks. In a hurry, we rushed out to the car.

Outside, Julia gave me a push before she ran to her car. Of course, she beat me to the car. Quickly jumping in, she started the engine before I could get in the door.

Before I could safely buckle up, the squeal of tires could be heard as she made her getaway. Julia drove wildly to the apartment building, where she slammed on her brakes and slid into a vacant parking space. In a hurry, after she stopped the car, she actually beat me to the gate.

Bowing, with a show of respect, I opened the gate. Immediately, she gave me another shove. Giggling, she raced up the stairs to her apartment. This time, I was ready for her and didn't let her beat me. Grabbing her ankle, she stumbled. Winded, she fell to her knees and dropped her keys.

"Damn it," she cried.

"Don't be in such a hurry," I told her.

"I think it was you who was racing with me," she teased.

"No, that had to be someone else."

Laughing, she said, "Let's have some good exercise before we head to the hot tub. Afterward, we can rush back to finish the night with more exercise before sleep."

"That sounds like a perfect plan."

In the bedroom, we quickly undressed. Even though I had seen her in a bikini, I couldn't wait to see her as naked as a J-bird and on the bed. After pulling off her clothes, she stood facing me, stark naked.

Staring at her breasts, I was in awe at their size. They were heavy but well-formed.   Her rosy red nipples stood out like ripe cherries. Letting my eyes drop to her hips and waist, I couldn't help but notice the hair between those luscious thighs matched the hair on her head.   A sudden rush to taste her was driving me crazy with need.   What a beautiful sight.   Now, in a hurry, I quickly rid myself of the rest of my clothes.   I was already erect.

"Jesus," she cried, "Will that fit?"

"Of course, it will fit."

Then Julia turned to the bed.   As she moved, I got a great view of her perfectly shaped bottom.   Everything about her was perfect.   On the bed, she laid back and with a smile, opened her arms and licked her lips.

"Come here for some enjoyment," she cooed.

Quickly sliding onto the bed, I took her into my arms. I started by giving her a blistering kiss.   In seconds, our kisses quickly turned into white hot passion.   Moving between her open thighs, I slid my hands beneath her. Grasping her curvy bottom, I lifted her from the mattress.

Placing her legs over my shoulders, I began teasing her beyond reason by kissing her in the folds. She screamed.   After a few minutes of teasing, I couldn't wait any longer.   She had already had a series of climaxes.

Letting her settle onto the mattress, I unmercifully began pushing the head of my erection back and forth over and around the lips of her vagina.

"Jesus H Christ," she screamed.

Her body began bucking and shaking uncontrollably. She closed her eyes and moaned.   Her head kept rolling on the pillow.

"You bastard," she moaned, "Please stop teasing me. I need to feel you in me, stretching me."

Laughing, I kept teasing her in the same fashion. Each time I paused at her opening, she tried raising her hips to capture my erection. I let it sink inside her just a fraction before pulling it away.

"God damn you," she moaned.

Eventually, needing to end the teasing, I stopped. Gently, I pushed a little further inside the opening. Feeling her tight wetness, I took her slowly. Every inch was enough to make me groan. Giving her another inch, but all of it, made her go wild. Finally, when I had just about all of it inside, I gave a final thrust. At that time, the movement of her hips made me thrust harder.

Buried to the hilt, Julia quickly locked her arms and legs around my body. Her movements triggered my climax. I tried pulling out, but her restraint stopped me.

"Holly shit," she cried, "I have never been fucked like this before."

"And we aren't done yet," I told her, "But first we need some fuel."

With our energy sapped, we rolled from the bed. We groaned as we stood and began to dress.

"This is crazy, why don't we order in?" I said.

"That is something I would like," Julia uttered.

"What would you like?" he asked.

"Pizza."

"You order what you want," I told her.

After the order was placed, we turned to face each other. Our yearning sent us into a clinch. Quickly, our kissing and fondling rekindled our passion. Knowing we had to hold off our passion until after the Pizza had arrived wasn't easy.

"We have to wait for the pizza," I said, releasing her, "otherwise it will get here while we are otherwise occupied and get cold."

"Staying away from you isn't easy either," Julia said, "After what we just did, I don't know how long I can wait for the next time."

Wearing robes provided by the motel, we wait impatiently for the Pizza to arrive. When it finally came, we were only able to eat two pieces a piece, before rushing back to the bed.

She didn't have to pull me very hard. In bed, she pushed me to my back. As I lay there, watching her move over me, I was enjoying the view.

Sitting in me, she smiled, then lifted her hips. Grasping me, she put me at my wet opening. This time, my penetration was easier. Sinking on my erection, she groaned. Once she was seated, she began riding me as if she were riding a horse.

Her movements were wild. She pushed down on me like she couldn't get all of me inside her. She must have climaxed two or three times before she planted her body on me. The way she planted herself, I knew I'd have to climax inside her.

We climaxed together.

FORTY-FIVE

BRUCE

The alarm woke me from a deep sleep. Springing from the bed, I realized there was only time for a quick shower. As I dressed, Julia looked at me.

"Will I see you tonight?" she asked.

"I hope so," I told her.

With enough time for one last kiss, I hurried out the door. Not able to get Julia out of my mind, I knew I had put myself in a bad situation. Under these circumstances, I really didn't care. Julia is married, and she keeps telling me what we are doing isn't for a long commitment. I knew that when her husband came home, she would go with him.

Driving to work, I hoped to divert all negative thoughts going through my brain. It worked for a while, but eventually, mostly at night, I couldn't help but dwell on the night we spent together. She had me bewitched. I couldn't forget her.

I had trouble concentrating on my job. All through the day, thoughts of her kept occupying my mind. The way her husband treated her, I didn't give a rat's ass about what her husband felt. Hell, I couldn't remember his name.

Once work was over, I left the base and drove to the apartment. Entering the gate, my eyes first traveled to the second floor, where Julia's apartment was. My mind and body were in turmoil. Wanting to be with her all the time was scary.   As badly as I wanted her, I had to fight my temptation.

"Are you looking for someone?" she said.

Glancing toward the pool, I saw the most beautiful woman looking at me.   She was just getting off the lounge.   As she made her way toward me, I stared at the yellow two-piece bathing suit covering her body.   Just looking at her made my heart beat wildly.   I remembered what her body looked like without that bikini.   With each step, her large breasts jiggled, and her long legs made her rounded hips move with grace.   Memories of last night drew me to her.

"Yes," I said, "I was looking for you."

"As you can see, you found me."

"Let me change, and I'll meet you at the hot tub?"

"Not on your life.   I'm going with you while you change," she told me.

Walking straight to me, she grabbed my hand and smiled.   Just the movement of her body was enough to drive me wild.   Everything about her drove me wild.   Ignoring her hands, I wrapped my arms around her and kissed her.

"Oh my," she cried, "we had better hurry."

Without hesitation, we rushed into my apartment.   Inside, we raced to the bedroom where I quickly undressed.   By the time I was undressed, Julia, wearing only her yellow bikini, was already naked and on the bed waiting for me.

Taking a deep breath, I swallowed the lump in my throat.   There was no foreplay.   Neither of us wanted nor needed it.   We made our connection quickly.   Our rhythm was instant.   It was as if we had been having sex together for years.   We made love slow and tantalizing.   With the sounds of our passion filling the air, the bed kept banging against the wall.   As we climaxed together, we collapsed, gripping each other tightly.

"My God, you make me feel fantastic," she cried.

"You give me the same satisfaction," I whispered.

Getting out of the bed, we put on our bathing suits. We strolled hand in hand to the Jacuzzi, not caring who saw us. Julia began to giggle.

"What is so funny?" I asked.

"The way your bed kept hitting the wall, everyone had to know what we were doing."

"It was sort of loud, wasn't it?"

Sliding into the Jacuzzi, we sat close together, holding hands.

"This is so crazy, Julia," I whispered.

"I know, but I can't help myself either."

"You're so bewitching," I told her.

"God, why do I have a husband?"

"You met him before you met me," I told her.

"Bruce, what do you really think about me?"

"You are gorgeous and someone I love being with. If circumstances were different, I'm sure things would be different between us."

"I know they would," she sighed, "But by all good conscience, I can't hurt Henry. He was my first love, and I guess, in one way, I still do love him."

FORTY-SIX

BRUCE

"What do you want out of life, Julia?" I asked.

"All I've ever wanted was a good husband, a happy marriage and a couple kids. When I married Henry, I thought I had all that, minus the kids."

"And now?"

"And now, I have found a man who has turned my world upside down," she said.

"If I were to get out of your life, would you be able to forget me?"

"I don't know if I will ever forget you. You are going to be part of my life forever. All I can say is, I don't want to lose you, even after Henry comes home."

"Then what?"

"I'll go with him if he still wants me."

"Why wouldn't he? He would be a fool not to want you."

"Because I really don't know how my feelings for you are going to affect me then."

"Look, I don't want to be the person who ruined your marriage. In the end, you would resent me," I said.

"Would you like it if I moved in with you?"

"Are you serious?"

"Yes. I don't want to be away from you, even for a short period of time," she said, "I couldn't stand seeing you every day and not be able to enjoy all you give me."

"I'd miss you too, Julia," I said, kissing her.

"Then, I will move in with you."

"I think it best that you don't move everything," I told her, "Maintain your apartment as if you're still living there."

"Why?"

"What will you do with all your things?"

"Store them," she said.

"And what would you tell your husband when comes home?"

"I would get them out before he comes home."

"And how will you explain why you moved to a different apartment if you can get another one?"

Taking a deep breath, she said, "Maybe you're right."

That night, we became roommates. The move took a few hours of our time. After she had everything she needed for everyday use, we were finally together.

With Julia in my life, I didn't need another woman. Once she left with her husband, I would worry about finding someone to take her place. But definitely not until then.

Julia and I quickly got used to each other. It was like we were actually married. She would be there for me, have dinner ready, and the apartment clean. Nights were a pure joy. Only two other women made me this happy, but neither of them was with me full-time like Julia.

Three months later, Julia gave me the news.

"You're going to be a daddy, Bruce."

"How along are you?"

"I must have gotten pregnant to first week after we met."

"How are you going to explain this to Henry?"

"I'll tell him the baby is his. He will believe me."

"Is that what you want?" I asked.

"No, but that is the way it has to be. When the doctor told me I was pregnant, I got a P.O. box number. When I leave, I want to keep in touch with you, so you can see how our child are growing."

"Julia, as much as I would love to hear from you and see the progress of our child, I don't think it wise. It might not ever happen, but we would be taking the chance on getting caught."

"How could I get caught?"

"All it would take is one time for Henry to accidentally find the proof," I told her.

"Well, if he finds out, I will come to you, if you still want me."

"I will always welcome you home. In my heart, your place will always be with me."

FORTY-SEVEN

JULIA

In my own apartment, I stood just inside the door to swoon. My body felt fantastic. My brain was another thing. It kept telling me I was being bad, and I guess I knew. Weighing my options, I found at this moment in my life, I really didn't care. Never have I ever been so happy or felt as good as I was feeling right now.

"Julia, as much as I would love to hear from you and see the progress of our child, I don't think it wise. We would be taking a big chance on getting caught."

"How could we get caught?"

"All it would take is one time for Henry to accidentally find the proof," he told me.

"Well, if he finds out, I will come to you, if you still want me."

"I will always welcome you home. In my heart, your place will always be with me."

To keep Bruce out of my mind, I kept myself busy by stripping our bed, washing and drying the sheets, then remaking the bed. Smiling, I thought, now we will have clean sheets.

After vacuuming the entire apartment, I began dusting. As the day moved on, I noticed I had cleaned my entire apartment. The apartment was cleaned much better than I had ever cleaned it before. Sighing, I suddenly felt exhausted. Laying on the couch for a short nap, it only took seconds to fall asleep.

Something made my eyes pop open. Glancing at the clock, I saw I had slept more than one hour. That was something I never did. Last night was so overpowering that I couldn't stay awake. Now that I was awake, my thoughts went directly to Bruce. What was it about Bruce that I couldn't get him out of my mind?

Glancing at the clock again, I saw there was at least an hour before Bruce came home. Should I go to him, the moment he comes through the door, or wait to see if he comes to me? Not used to this new life, I was constantly wondering, do I really satisfy him as much as he satisfies me? I don't know if that was possible.

I couldn't wait to see him when he came through the door, from where he had been. Then again, I would love to be at the pool, to see what he does. God, one night with him and I felt like I didn't want anything else. I had never felt this excited about any man before. Jumping into bed with him, the same night my husband left home, was astonishing.

Wanting to be in the right place, I hurried to the pool. Taking a lounge where I could see when he came in, I tried to get comfortable. No such luck. Then, about five minutes later, he walked in. He was looked up to where I was living. That was what told me he was looking for me.

"Are you looking for someone?" I asked.

Getting off the lounge, I made my way toward him. The way he was looking at me made my heart beat wildly. With each step I took towards him, memories of last night drew me to him.

"Yes," he said, "I was looking for you."

"As you can see, you found me."

His eyes bore into me as he said, "Let me change, and I'll meet you at the hot tub?"

"Not on your life. I'm going with you while you change," I told him.

Walking straight to him, I grabbed his hand and smiled. Ignoring my hands, he wrapped his arms around me and kissed me.

"Oh my, we had better hurry," I cried.

Without hesitation, we rushed into his apartment. It was a race to the bedroom. With not as much to take off as he, I was undressed and on the bed waiting for him.

After last night, we didn't need foreplay. When he slid into me, I thought I would die. It was quick and smooth. We quickly found a rhythm. It was as if we had been having sex for years. We moved slowly together. We got the most wonderful enjoyment out of being together. Sounds of passion filled the air as the bed banged against the wall. After climaxing, we collapsed, gripping each other tightly.

"My God, you make me feel fantastic," I cried.

"You give me the same satisfaction," he whispered.

Getting out of the bed, we dressed in our bathing suits. Strolling hand in hand to the Jacuzzi, not caring who saw us, I began to giggle.

"What is so funny?" he asked.

"The way your bed kept hitting the wall, everyone had to know what we were doing."

"It was sort of loud, wasn't it?"

Sliding into the Jacuzzi, we sat close together, holding hands.

FORTY-EIGHT

BRUCE

"This is so crazy, Julia," he whispered.

"I know, but I can't help myself either."

"You're so bewitching," he told me.

"God, why do I have a husband?"

"You met him before you met me," he told me.

"Bruce, what do you really think about me?"

"You are gorgeous and someone I love being with. If circumstances were different, I'm sure, things would be different between us."

"I know they would," I sighed, "But by all good conscience, I can't hurt Henry. He was my first love, and I guess in one way, I still do love him."

"What do you want out of life, Julia?" Bruce asked.

"All I've ever wanted is a good husband, a happy marriage and a couple kids to raise. When I married Henry, I thought I had all that, minus the kids."

"And now?"

"And now I have found a man who has turned my world upside down," I said.

"You met him before you met me," he told me.

"Bruce, what do you really think about me?"

"You are gorgeous and someone I love being with. If circumstances were different, I'm sure, things would be different between us."

"I know they would," I sighed, "But by all good conscience, I can't hurt Henry. He was my first love, and I guess in one way, I still do love him."

"What do you want out of life, Julia?" Bruce asked.

"All I've ever wanted is a good husband, a happy marriage and a couple kids to raise. When I married Henry, I thought I had all that, minus the kids."

"And now?"

"And now I have found a man who has turned my world upside down," I said.

"If I were to get out of your life, would you be able to forget me?"

"I don't know if I will ever forget you. You are going to be part of my life forever. All I can say is, I don't want to lose you, even after Henry comes home."

"Then what?"

"I'll go with him, if he still wants me too."

"Why wouldn't he? He would be a fool not to want you."

"Because I really don't know how my feelings for you are going to affect me then."

"Look, I don't want to be the person who ruined your marriage. In the end, you would resent me," Bruce said.

"Would you like it if I moved in with you?"

"Are you serious?"

"Yes. I don't want to be away from you, even for a short period of time," I told him "I couldn't stand seeing you every day and not be able to enjoy all you give me."

"I'd miss you too, Julia," he said, kissing me.

"Then, I will move in with you."

"I think it best that you don't move everything," he told me "Maintain your apartment as if you're still living there."

"Why?"

"What will you do with all your things?"

"Store them," I said.

"And what would you tell your husband when comes home?"

"I would get them out before he comes home."

"And how will you explain why you moved to a different apartment, if you can get another one?"

Taking a deep breath, I said, "Maybe you're right."

FORTY-NINE

BRUCE

That night, we became real roommates. The move took a few hours of our time. After I had everything I would need for everyday use, we were finally together.

Bruce and I quickly got used to each other. It was like we were actually married. I made sure I was home with dinner ready and clean. Nights were pure pleasure. Three months later, I dropped the bomb.

When the doctor told me I was pregnant, I got a P.O. box number. When I leave, I want to keep in touch with you, so you can see how our child are growing."

"Julia, as much as I would love to hear from you and see the progress of our child, I don't think it wise. We would be taking the chance on getting caught."

"How could I get caught?"

"All it would take is one time for Henry to accidentally find the proof," he told me.

"Well, if he finds out, I will come to you, if you still want me."

"I will always welcome you home. In my heart, your place will always be with me."

When Bruce told me that I would always have a home with him, I got completely confused. My heart and my body wanted different things.

My mind sat to stay with Bruce and remain happy, but my heart says I couldn't hurt Henry that way.

It was a difficult decision, but I made my bed; now, as much as I don't want to, I would have to lie in it.

FIFTY

JULIA

The day Henry came home, I was ready to deliver. Henry wasn't the happiest man in the world about the baby. It seems he wasn't ready to be a father. While Henry was home, I did my best to ignore Bruce, but found it very difficult. I knew our time together was over, but I now have a large problem, I already to miss Bruce terribly.

One week before Henry and I were ready to leave, I went into labor. Knowing the child was Bruce's, and knowing he wasn't supposed to be around me any longer, didn't mean anything to him. Taking a huge chance, he came to the hospital to see his child anyway. There was no way he could stay away, no matter how much he wanted to. I had given birth to his son, whom I named Joshua.

"What are you doing here, Bruce?" Henry snarled.

"I wouldn't be here at all, except Julia and I are good friends," Bruce told Henry.

Knowing I was having his child, he wanted to at least be the friend he was to me, while Henry was away and give the baby a gift."

"Okay," Henry grumbled, "You can say hi, but then you have to go."

"Thanks, Henry," Bruce said, "I hear your moving home. I hope the three of you have a good and happy life together."

"We will once we get away from this place," Henry said.

"When do you expect to leave?"

"I get discharged in one week. I'm hoping to get away shortly after that."

Stepping past Henry, Bruce entered the room. I was sitting up in the bed, holding our child. Still not trusting me, Henry stood in the doorway to watch our every move.

"Hi Julia," Bruce whispered.

Going to the far side of the bed, Bruce handed me the gift.

"You have a beautiful baby boy," Bruce said," Here is a gift I brought for the baby. I hope you have a good life, wherever you are going."

"Thanks, Bruce," I said.

When I touched his hand, I had a hard time stifling the sadness I was feeling.

FIFTY-ONE

BRUCE

Knowing this would be the last time I would ever see Julia again, sadness enveloped me. On the drive home from the hospital, I was tempted to turn around and tell Henry the truth, but I couldn't do that to Julia.

At the apartment, I changed into my bathing suit and went to the Jacuzzi to relax. The Jacuzzi wasn't the same without Julia being with me. A few other people were already there. In a way, I was grateful for the company.

Life changed for me with Julia gone. Getting buried in my work, I didn't date. The way I was feeling, dating for me was a thing of the past. I couldn't get Julia out of my mind.

Then my mind drifted to Lana. What was she doing? How was she getting along?

Then thinking of Delores, the beautiful black girl, I could have been happy with. Damn, I have met three incredible women. Two of them were married, and the other couldn't handle an interracial relationship. Was I destined to meet only women I couldn't have a good relationship with?

"What's wrong, Bruce?" Harry, a guy I work with, asked.

"What makes you think something is wrong?"

"You seemed to have changed," Harry said, "You used to be talkative and have a sense of humor. Now you don't screw around any longer."

"Since you are a good guy, Harry, I'll tell you. I had been living with a woman I can't get out of my mind. She was married, and her husband came home. He took his discharge, and she left with him."

"So, you fell for the woman, huh?"

"Yes. She was one hell of a woman."

"There are other women in this world."

I remembered telling that to my mother when Lana and I went different ways.

"I know. After some time, I'll adjust and look again."

Later that night, as I was watching a ball game on television, thoughts of Lana and Julia returned. Being I was twenty-nine, Lana had to be forty-two. By now, one of her daughters has to be married.

Let's see, if my math is right, the married daughter should be twenty-two. I wonder if she has any children yet. Now the youngest one must be nineteen, old enough for college.

Then I met Julia. Her age has to be twenty-two. That is quite a coincidence. Our son was almost six months old. To think I have been in the military for eleven years. Another nine and I could retire.

The next day, Harry introduced me to his wife, Michelle. Michelle was a cute, tiny, auburn-haired baby doll. With her was her best friend, Abigail.

"Bruce, this is my wife Michelle and her friend Abigail."

"Hello girls."

"Hi," they said.

On a guess, Abigail stood five four or five. She was petite and a very attractive blond. The two girls looked to be around twenty.

"Michelle and I want to invite you to our house for dinner."

"I'd like that," I told him, "I haven't had a home-cooked meal in ages."

When we got to their place, I learned Abigail was only eighteen and Michelle's cousin.   Abigail was in her freshman year at the university in town.

As Harry helped Michelle with the dinner, Abigail sat with me in the living room.

"How long have you been in the military, Bruce?"

"Ten years," he told her.

"I've been told you have never married."

"That is true.   I guess I haven't found the right woman yet."

"I thought Harry said you had been living with a married woman in town."

"Yes, that is true also.   The woman and her husband lived in the same apartment complex I do.   When her husband went overseas, I sort of took over for him."

"Was she pretty?"

"She was very beautiful."

"Did she go with her husband when he left here?"

"Yes."

"Are in the market?" she asked.

"I'm sorry, but I am not.   Yet."

"If you let me, maybe I can change your mind.   I'm looking for a male friend."

"You are very pretty, Abigail, but you about eleven years younger than I am."

"Call me Abby."

"Okay, Abby, but you are a little young for me, don't you think?"

"What is the youngest girl you would date?"

"Twenty-one."

"I'm eighteen, but if you give me a chance, I could act older than my age, to be with you."

"Do you live in the Dorm?"

"No, I have my own apartment."

"How can you afford your own place?"

"My dad is paying. Why don't you come over to look at the place? You might like it."

"You're a little forward, aren't you?" I asked.

"My parents always said, if you want something, go for it. If you don't and you will lose it, you have no one to blame but yourself."

"Your parents sound like interesting people," I said, "Why haven't you gone for guys more your age?"

"To begin, with I like older men."

"What is it that makes you want an older man?"

"While we are on the subject, how old are you?" she asked.

"I'm twenty-nine."

"I can be interesting, if you give me a chance."

"You have spunk. I like that."

Abby handed me a card with her address and phone number on it.

"Dinner is ready," Michelle said from the doorway.

Abby went first. Michelle hung back.

"If you take her out, she will make you forget the woman you had been living with."

"After talking with Abby, I could tell she is street smart."

Michelle just chuckled.

When everyone was seated, we held hands while Abby gave grace. The meal was delicious and the company was great. When the meal was over, everyone sat to play cards. Around ten o'clock, the game ended.

"Thanks for dinner, Harry. I'll see you tomorrow."

"Would you walk me out, Bruce?" Abby asked.

FIFTY-TWO

BRUCE

The next day at work, Harry didn't say anything about the night before. Abby seemed like a great gal, but my heart was still torn. True, I had put myself in that position. I shouldn't have taken Julia out, no matter how much she stirred me.

It was the same with Lana, although I didn't pursue her. She had pursued me. Nevertheless, because both were married, I should not have been with them.

Every night, I went to bed in torment. I would wake up in a sweat. Memories of Lana and Julia didn't give me much rest. Lying in the dark, I would wonder what they were doing and how they were getting along. Were they really happy or not?

Two months

"Hey buddy, you're killing yourself. Call Abby. She has asked me several times how you are."

"Harry, she is one nice girl, but too young. I'm eleven years older, I'm fucked up and don't want to hurt her."

"Take her out," Harry said, "You don't have anything to lose. You don't have to kiss her. Just be with her for company. She understands where you are coming from. Abby hasn't been through what you have, but she did get hurt once by a guy she really liked. Ask her to dinner one time."

"Knowing what I have done, how can she want to put herself in that position?"

"Because she knows down deep you are a good guy," Harry said, "She feels the both of you can use each other to get over the hurt."

"Okay, I'll call her, but don't expect anything to happen."

"Hey, what happens between the two of you is on the two of you. I just see her helping you forget."

That night, I called her.

"Hello," she said, after the second ring.

"Hi, Abby, it's Bruce."

"Harry said you would call. How have you been?"

"I'm getting along, how about yourself?"

"Now that you called, I do feel better."

"I hope you aren't setting yourself up to get hurt," I told her.

"If I am, then I am," she sighed, "but I don't think you will hurt me purposely. Your issues are strong, but I think I can help you get over them."

"Look, I would much rather talk to you in person. Are you hungry?"

"I could use something to eat, but not a meal."

"How about I pick you up and take you to A&W. We can sit in the car and talk. No one will hear us, and we can say what we want. I have to tell you, I don't beat around the bush, so tell me now if you have changed your mind."

"No. I have not changed my mind. I like people who don't beat around the bush, as you say. Even if I don't like what you are saying, I will at least know where I stand."

"When will you be ready?"

"If you come now, I will be waiting outside."

Getting into my car, I sat for a moment contemplating whether I was doing the right thing or not. Starting the engine, I thought, it is too late to worry now, she will be waiting for me.

Arriving at her place, I found her leaning up a car. Stopping, I got out to open her door. She was wearing powder blue shorts and a blouse to match. Her dirty blond hair was in a ponytail, which made her look younger than eighteen. Once she was in and settled, I hurried back to the driver's side. As I took my seat behind the wheel, I glanced at her. A huge smile was spread across her pretty face.

"Hi," she said.

"What is so funny?"

"You. For a guy who thinks he is bad, you sure have a way of showing your good side."

"And how do I do that?"

"You treat a girl like a woman."

"I guess I do, it is out of habit," I told her.

"A guy who thinks of just himself would never think of doing anything for a girl."

Smiling, I drove away.

FIFTY-THREE

BRUCE

“We don’t have to go anywhere to talk,” she said.

“I’m not the type to dump on someone and not at least give them something to enjoy.”

“Hey, I’m going to dump on you too,” she said.

“All the more the reason to do something good.”

“I can see why Harry likes you.”

“Harry is a great guy.”

She laughed again.

Pulling into the A&W, I opened my window.

“What would you like?” I asked.

“Whatever you’re having, will be fine,” she said.

“Oh, I thought you said something lite?”

“What are you having?” she asked.

“Steak and Lobster.”

“You can’t get that here,” she said.

“I can’t?” I asked in a surprised tone, “What can I get here?”

“Oh, I get it,” she laughed, “you’re pulling my leg.”

"I wouldn't mind pulling that leg," I said, looking down, "Your leg is nicely shaped."

"I won't let you pull it on our first date," she laughed.

"Oh yeah, the girl does have a sense of humor."

"Being around you, a girl has to be prepared."

"Harry was right, you are special," I chuckled, "I'm already starting to enjoy myself."

"I'll take that as a compliment," she said.

When the girl came to the car on roller skates carrying our order, we stopped talking. When she was gone, I began again.

"Okay, Abigail."

"Whoa there," she said, "Are you my friend?"

"I'd like to be."

"Then you have to call me Abby."

"Okay, Abby. Tell me about yourself."

"I'm eighteen, single and talking to a nice guy."

"Okay, smarty, what are your interests?"

"Oh. What do I like to do?"

Looking at me, she tapped her finger on her chin. Then she smiled.

"Now you're being a smart ass," I teased back.

"No, I'm just giving you some of your own medicine."

"Let's be serious, for a moment," I said.

"I'm flexible," she said, "I'll do anything a guy likes to do, within reason."

"How do you know what I was thinking?"

"Harry gave me a good idea what you are like."

Laughing, I said, "Would you like to go fishing in a boat or take an overnight trip with me?"

"Yes. Both would be fun."

"Knowing what I have done, you can still trust me?"

"I don't think what you have done is all your fault. Those women wanted you, too."

"Oh, so you wouldn't want me?"

"Not right away. You have to work for what you want."

"Do you do anything on your own?"

"I play softball for the college."

"When is your next game?"

"Eleven o'clock Saturday morning."

"Where?"

"At the college."

"I'll be there."

"Are you kidding? I would love for you to be there."

"Then, I will be there."

"Do you play ball?" she asked.

"I haven't this year, but I used to be on two different teams in two different leagues."

"Well then, have you ever played co-ed?"

"No."

"Would you like to try?"

"Sure."

"I play on Wednesday nights, and we have just lost a player."

"You don't know how well I can play."

"I don't care. You are another player, and we need one. Your abilities will come back to you," she said.

We rattled on the entire night, even after the food was finished and gone. It was evident to both of us, we were really enjoying each other's company. Looking at the clock, I gasped.

"What time is your class tomorrow?" I asked.

"Nine."

"I would normally say you need beauty sleep, but I can't say that to you. You're not only beautiful to look at, you're beautiful to talk too."

"Watch it, you'll make my head swell," she laughed.

"I'm not trying to get rid of you, but are you ready to go back to your place?"

"I guess I am, I do have things to do before school tomorrow."

Pulling up to her apartment, I rushed around to let her out. It was wasted energy. She was standing there waiting her me. Stopping at a pleasant distance, I offered her my hand.

"No kiss?" she asked.

"You always say, not on your first date."

"I'll consider meeting you at Harry's was our first date."

Stepping forward, I placed my hands on the hips. The moment I touched her, she moaned as she placed her arms went around my neck. Her kiss was warm and gentle, and she tasted good.

After our first date, Abby became a steady girl to me. After hurting two women, I didn't want to make her the third, but my shore duty time was up. Receiving my orders, I went straight to Abby's apartment. Liking Abby a lot, I couldn't just leave and hang her out to dry. She still had three years of college, so I confronted her at her apartment. Entering, we immediately hugged and kissed before telling her the news.

"I have my orders, Abby."

"Where are you going?"

"Okinawa."

"I wish I could go with you," she said.

"I'll be gone nine months. If you are still available when I get back, maybe we can give this relationship another go."

"When are you leaving?"

"I leave for Pendleton in two weeks. I'll be gone two weeks, then go on deployment two weeks after that."

"Call me when you get back. I'll be waiting."

FIFTY-FOUR

BRUCE

“**F**or tonight, where do you want to go?” I asked.

“We have been dating for three months now,” Abby said, “Don’t you think we should make our relationship stronger?”

“What are you saying?”

“You have never tried to bed me,” she said, “Is there some reason you haven’t tried? Don’t I turn you on, or do you look at me just as a friend?”

“I haven’t tried bedding you, because I respect you too much, and I don’t want to hurt you.”

“It hurts me to think, I can’t get you horny enough, to at least try.”

“It is a little late now, isn’t it?   Hell, I’m leaving.”

“Other men leave their wives and girlfriends, but they have sex before they leave.”

“I guess you have me there.”

Grabbing my hands, she pulled me from the couch. With a smile, she turned toward her bedroom. I didn’t resist.

“I think, think this is the time for our relationship to grow,” she said.

The minute we entered her bedroom, she closed the door and then leaned against it.   A smile appeared on her face.

"Finally," she uttered.

In her bedroom, I wanted to do more, but all I could do was look at her.

"Are you going to spend the night?" she asked me.

"If that is what you want," I said, "I wouldn't want it any other way."

"Good, because that is what I want."

We undressed tantalizingly slow.   Naked, she was more beautiful than I imagined.   The clothes she wore didn't do her justice.   The only time I ever got a fair view was the few times I had seen her wearing shorts.   Naked, she was gorgeous.

"From the looks of it, I'm in for a real treat," she said.

Stepping over to me, she grasped my erection.

"Just be gentle," she said, "I've only done it once, and your size does tend to scare me."

"Abby, we are just getting started."

On the bed, we came together.   We started by cuddling.   Then, after a few minutes, we began kissing.   As we kissed, I began fondling her. My attentions were all new to Abby.   Using my hands and mouth, I did my best to teach her was good sex was all about.   Then I stopped.

"Tell me what your first time was like."

"It was disaster.   The guy was quick. I didn't have to get introduced, as you would say."

"This is going to be totally different.   Before we got started," I said, I took the time to roll on a rubber. She watched, "You need to be protected from pregnancy."

Then I brought her back into my arms. I started with gentle kisses and soft, tender fondling. It wasn't long before I felt her coming alive.

"Ooooh," she moaned.

Kissing my way down to her breasts, I captured one, then the other nipple in my mouth. Immediately, her head began turning on the pillow. Her breathing had become ragged. It wasn't long before her hips began lifting from the bed. Not finished yet, I kissed my way down to rim her belly button.

Finding her limp, I lifted her legs over my shoulders. When I had her in position, I buried his face in her vagina. She screamed once, then twice. After her second scream, I kissed his way up her body again. Stopping at her breasts, I aimed my erection at her vagina. Inserting the tip, just inside the lips of her womanhood, I held still.

"My God, Bruce, you're driving me wild."

"You're driving me wild, too," I told her.

"Then what are you waiting for?" she cried.

With me, already just inside her opening, to hold me in place, she quickly wrapped her legs around my waist. She acted like she knew what she was doing; she squeezed her legs around my waist.

"Ooooh, my Gooood," she cried out.

I wanted to sink into her inch by inch. With her legs tightly around my waist, I had no choice but to bury myself to the hilt. She screamed several times until I was completely in. Her tightness quickly had me on the brink. Not wanting this to end so quickly, I tried to withdraw. Her legs wouldn't allow that. I was doomed.

"This first time is going to be short," I told her.

She screamed again.

"My God, I'm coming again," she moaned.

Grunting, I gave her everything I had. I was glad I was wearing protection.

Out of breath, we remained connected. A few moments later, when she lowered her legs to the bed, I was able to roll from her.

"That was fantastic," she cried.

"You sure know how to make a man happy," I told her.

"I'm going to miss you," she said, "Please come over every night until you leave?"

"After what you just gave me, there is no way I would miss being in your bed every night."

For the next two weeks, we lived together. Then I was off to training. In those two weeks I she was always on my mind. Also, during those two weeks, the woman was insatiable. The question now was, will she crave sex so bad that will she wait?

Abby met me at the airport when I came home. She acted as if I had been gone a year. Missing her hugs and kisses, we didn't waste any time getting to her apartment. We were hot the two weeks before training, now we were at each other constantly. The woman couldn't get enough.

Harry and Michelle had us over for dinner once. When Abby wasn't in school, she studied hard. Harry had been right. Abby had the ability to take my mind off my past.

Our relationship quickly became fluid, as if we had been married for years. Because of Abby, I didn't have eyes for other women. Feeling comfortable with me, Abby vowed to remain faithful also.

Abby went to the airport with me the day I was to deploy. As did the married couples, we hugged and kissed. When we parted, she cried. The flight seemed to take longer than normal.

We wrote three times a week.   Three months into my deployment, tragedy took me by surprise.   My parents had been killed in an auto accident.   Taking emergency leave, I flew home.

Fifty-Five

BRUCE

As soon as my plane landed in Connecticut, I called Abby.

"Hey Abby, I'm in Connecticut."

"What are you doing there?"

"My parents were killed in an auto accident. I will be remaining here until everything is taken care of."

"Do you want me to join you?"

"That isn't necessary, just finish your studies. When this is over, I will be flying back to Okinawa."

"Oh, I see," she said, in a hurt tone."

"Do I hear annoyance?"

"Well, yes, I would like to be with you."

"And I want to be with you too, but I will be very busy and need time to adjust to my loss."

"I don't like it, but I do understand," she told me.

"I miss you. I'll call you in a couple days when this is over and I fly back to Okinawa."

"I miss you," she said, and hung up.

Hanging up, I went to the funeral home, where preparations were being completed.   At the end of the day, I went back to the cottage. Now that the cottage was mine.   I had to make a choice.   Should I sell this cottage, or fix it up for all-year-round living?

If I was to keep the cottage, with seven more years to serve, I would have to rent the place out.   If sold it, how long would it take to sell? With a thousand questions filling my head, I walked out on the dock. Looking out over the water, I made a quick decision.   Still loving this place, I didn't really want to lose it.

Having made up my mind, I knew what I had to do to make it into a year-round home.   I had always wanted my parents to renovate the cottage, but my dad had been adamant about not spending the money.

Now that I owned the place, I would have plans drawn up on how I wanted the place to look like when it was completed.   Of course, since I won't be living there until I retire, my plans for the renovation will be on hold till then.   Meanwhile, I will need a real estate company to rent the place until that time.

Fifty-Six

BRUCE

I finished my tour in Okinawa, and Abby was waiting for my return. Three months later, I was off the Guam.   Nine months in Guam seemed to long for Abby and I; from Guam, it was back to Okinawa.

Time flew by.   At the age of thirty-seven, I was ready to retire.   What little shore duty I had didn't make up for all the times I was gone nine months a year.

I didn't have time to begin the upper floor before I left.   I was thirty now and knew I had begun this project for my future.   Once I was retired from the military, I wanted to come back to live here year-round. I was assuming Abby would come with me.

I called Abby several times during the next three weeks, mentioning my plans.   As it turned out, Abby wasn't too happy about my plans.   She wouldn't mind visiting the lake, but didn't want to live there.   Her family expected her to move to their area.   That was the beginning of the end for us.

When he got back from my deployment, Abby and I rekindled our relationship.   The first few days were spent catching up on lost time.

"Do you really want to move to Connecticut?" she asked.

"Yes.   We will live by the lake in a small, peaceful town that is very quiet."

"I don't think it will be us," she said.

"Why do you say that?"

"I had plans long before we met. In my mind and heart, I don't think I want to change them."

"Abby, you have two more years of college, and I have eight more years of service."

"Eight years is a long time, Bruce. Do you expect me to live here alone after I graduate?"

"I had that in mind," I told her.

"Why don't we play this by ear and see how it works?"

"Being I have two more deployments to do before I got shore duty again, we needed to make a final decision on how we wanted to handle this relationship."

"What are your feelings?" she asked.

"I'm hoping something will change in the next two years before you graduate."

"So, we'll live together when you are home, then before I graduated, we will come to a definite decision."

"If that is what you want," I said.

"Okay," she said.

Our time together, while I was home, was as good as it always was. We waited on each other and enjoyed being together. Our happiest times were when we slept together and woke in the morning to start the day off with good sex.

When it was time for me to leave, Abby cried. The promise to write three days a week remained the same. For the entire next two years, they remained faithful to each other. I attended Abby's graduation. After the ceremony, we went to dinner. Abby was all smiles.

"Did you find a job yet?" I asked.

“Hey, I just graduated.   Give me time.”

“I guess I asked, so I know if you intend to stay with me or go.”

“I’m leaning on going, but my heart tells me it would be a mistake.”

“I’m due for shore duty in another year.”

“Are you asking me to stay?”

“Do I need too?”

She was quiet for a moment.   I didn’t like the look on her face.   She was still trying to decide.   To me, that wasn’t a good sign.

“I’m going to miss you, Abby.”

“I haven’t decided yet,” she said.

“Yes, you have, but you’re hoping in the last minute I’ll change my mind.”

“I know you can’t go now.   I’m torn,” she said, “If I go, I could regret the move.   On the other hand, I need a job.   Around this area, jobs don’t look too promising.”

That night we slept together as we always did, but the tension was so great neither of us were in the mood for sex.   The next morning, Abby rolled to face me.

“Make love to me for the last time, Bruce.”

The next day, after work, I found Abby had packed and was gone.

FIFTY-SEVEN

Going on thirty-three, I felt like I had been pushed through a ringer. Abby actually left me. This was my time to feel hurt. Having screwed over two guys by having affairs with their wives, maybe I deserved what I was now getting. The only woman I had been with who wasn't married was doing what she wanted to do. Now I was alone.

What was I going to do for the next five years? Hoping to forget about my troubles, I decided I needed a change of scenery. Taking a month's leave, I flew home. It seems the agency taking care of my property was having trouble renting the house. It would be a good time for me to go home. I had to see what the construction crew had done to my cottage, or should I say my home now that it has been weatherized.

Needing time away from my everyday life, I made the trip home. I told the agency my plans. My flight didn't leave until midnight. Driving to the airport, I left my car in long-term parking. Boarding the plane, I found my seat was next to a middle-aged woman with a girl who looked to be ten or twelve years old.

Then the thought came to me. The way I was living my life, will I ever have children? Finding the right girl, after having three beauties and letting them go, won't be easy. Normally, finding two good women is hard enough, let alone four. Who knows what life will bring? After I retire in five years, I will just move back to my new home by the lake.

Sleeping most of the journey helped me relax a little. I was lucky the young girl sitting next to me wasn't any trouble. I talked a little with the mother and her daughter once we were in the air. As we landed, the young girl told me they lived in Hartford.   From the airport, I had another two-hour drive home.

It was early morning when I rented the car. The heat of the day had yet to climb higher. Yet, humidity hung in the air like a wet blanket. It made me feel as if I were in a shower. My only hope was that the lake would be cooler. Two hours later, after arriving in town, I stopped at the agency.

"How are you, Mr. Benson?"

"I'm fine, George, how have things been going?"

"Your house is ready for you, sir."

"Please don't call me sir. You make me feel old."

George laughed as he handed me the keys.

"I'll be turning these in when I leave," I told him.

"Very good," George said.

Driving to the house, I couldn't get over the beauty before me.   I had forgotten how beautiful the lake was. Pulling into the parking space, I grabbed my bag, then walked around the house, gazing at it as I went. The home looked much bigger compared to how I remembered it. The extra room for the hot tub had made a huge difference.

Dropping my bag on the porch, I walked out onto the dock. Gazing down into the water, I couldn't help but remember when I was younger. Fishing from the dock for sunfish was something I always had fun doing. My dad always made me throw them back. Not only were they too bony to eat, but they also helped keep the sand on the bottom clean.

Smiling, I turned back to the house. Picking up my bag, I unlocked the door to step inside. The job I had done on the first floor, the last time I was home, looked good. Climbing the stairs to the second floor, my first stop was the master bedroom. The sight was quite difference.

Sliding glass doors took the place of the window that viewed the lake. Opening the sliding doors, I could see that the hot tub would make the bedroom steamy with the doors open. The outside wall of the Jacuzzi room had removable windows for summer use.

Opening the windows in the Jacuzzi room, I turned on the heat to the tub. To keep the bedroom cool, I closed the bedroom door. Gazing out over the lake, I found the view absolutely gorgeous. Turning on the lights, the room took on a dim texture. Satisfied with the remodeling, I turned off the light and left.

Needing lunch supplies, I drove to the only grocery store in town. For a small town, the store was huge, carrying everything anyone would need. Grabbing a cart, I began searching each aisle. Not paying attention as I rounded a corner, I banged my cart into another cart. Startled, the woman pushing the other cart screamed and dropped what she had in her hands.

"Oh, I'm so sorry," I cried, "I wasn't paying attention to where I was going."

"No, it wasn't all your fault," she said, "I was preoccupied too."

The woman seemed very young, and her smile was infectious. Long blond hair surrounded her gorgeous face. She was probably a few inches short of my six-three frame.

"My name is Bruce; may I ask you yours?"

She chuckled, then said, "Miranda."

"It is nice to meet you, Miranda, even if it wasn't in the best fashion."

Bowing her head, she gave off with that pretty laugh again.

Moving aside, I let her pass. I couldn't help but let my eyes travel over her. Not only was she beautiful, but her walk was sexy as hell. Wearing light blue shorts, I got a great view of her long, shapely legs, a round bottom and the sexy swing of her hips. She was the same type of woman I gave up and lost.

Completing my shopping, I moved on to the check stand. The woman I bumped into was just ahead of me in line. She seemed to be in another world, so I didn't speak to her.   At the checkout stand, my opportunity came.   She was short on money.

"I'll put this back, she said.

"No, don't," I told her, "I'll cover it."

"Why would you do that?   You don't know me."

"We did sort of meet and I caused the accident," he said, "So it isn't like we are total strangers."

"We did meet that way, didn't we.   Back in the aisle, even if it were an accident."

"Let me pay, it isn't that much," I told her.

"Thank you," she said.

After going through the line, Miranda waited until I was done.

FIFTY-EIGHT

s I left the cashier, Miranda walked over to me.

"That was very nice of you," Miranda said, "But you didn't have to do that."

"I know I didn't have to, but I wanted too," I said, smiling, "Just consider it as being helpful."

We walked together to the parking lot, only to be surprised at how close we had parked to each other.

"Look, I know this is sort of out of place," I said, "but now that we have met, I would like to get to know you better. That is, if you are not married or engaged."

I enjoyed hearing her laugh. It was melodious and added to her beauty. When she didn't answer right away, I took it as her answer would be no.

"I'm sorry, I shouldn't have asked," I said suddenly.

Turning to my car, I began unloading my cart. A sudden movement and a whiff of lavender permeated the air.

"I would love to have lunch with you," she told me.

"What changed your mind?" I asked.

"I didn't change my mind, I just wanted to be sure I wasn't going to miss something."

"Do you have any place you prefer?" I asked.

"Yes," she said, "As a matter of fact, there is a nice cafe overlooking the lake not far from here."

"That sounds perfect.   I'm buying, of course."

"As you wish," she said.

Getting to our own vehicles, I followed her to the small cafe.   The cafe sat on stilts over the water.   Boats were parked beneath it.   Walking through the cafe, she led me to a wooden patio over the lake.   Several tables with umbrellas decorated the Patio.

"Hi Miranda," the man said.

"Hello Charles.   A table for two on the patio, please," she said.

Charles led the way.   The table he chose had a great view of the lake.

"Thanks, Charles," she said.

"Anything for you, Miranda," he said.

Holding her chair, I waited until she was comfortable before pushing her under the table.   Taking me seat across from her, I gave her a smile she would like.

"Tell me about yourself," I said.

"There isn't much to tell.   I have a mother, I don't see very often and a married sister, who is living in another state.   As for me, I live in a nice apartment with my best friend.   Is there anything else?"

"What do you do for work, and is your roommate male or female?"

"My roommate is a woman and I'm in my last year of teachers college."

"What subjects do you want to teach?"

"I'd like to teach grade school," she said.

"Just looking at you, I can see you will make a fantastic teacher."

"Thank you, now about you."

"What do you want to know?"

"Are you married, engaged or otherwise entangled?"

"No on all three. But I do have to admit, I have been in three relationships that I loved to be in, but circumstances prevented those relationships from growing."

"Where are you from?" she asked.

"I was born and raised right here in Connecticut. I'm in the military at the moment and still have five years before I can retire."

"Where do you want to live once you retire?"

"My parents died last year. They owned a cottage at the lake, which I converted into a winter home."

"Are you the person who redone the house by the park?"

"Guilty as charged."

"I'd love to see what you did with that place."

"If you have time after we eat, I can give you a tour."

"No, I'm sorry, but I have something I have to do today. But if you will be home tomorrow, I'd love to come over tomorrow with my friend to see the place."

"You and your friend will be welcome to come whenever you want. I have a hot tub, so bring a suit."

"We will do that and we will supply lunch."

"I have plenty of food," I told her.

"I insist," she said.

"You win," I said, raising my hands in defeat, "I don't like arguing, especially with a beautiful woman."

"I have a feeling you are at least ten years older than me," she said.

"Is that a bad thing?"

"No, I was just thinking."

"That could be dangerous," I said jokingly.

"Oh, I can see you and I will get along fabulously. The man has a sense of humor."

"Yes, and it is a warped humor."

"All the better," she chuckled, "Beware, I can get aggressive."

"Bring it on," I chuckled.

"Look, I'd love to keep this going, but as I said, I have things to do, but I will be at your place tomorrow."

"I'll be expecting you."

Before getting into my own car, I made sure she was settled in her car. She drove away in a direction opposite to where I was going. Not much later, I was unloading my car and stocking my pantry. Knowing Miranda and her friend would be coming tomorrow, I had a lot of work to do to make the place presentable.

Stocking the refrigerator, I moved on to the living room. With the living room completed, my next job were the bedrooms. I checked the other two bedrooms to be sure they were clean and the beds were made. From there to my bedroom, I unpacked my clothes and hung everything up that needed hanging.

By the time I was done, it was nearing three o'clock. Hot and tired, I wanted to slip into my hot tub stark naked to relax. Before that, I made a trip to the kitchen. Taking a bottle of beer from the fridge, I stepped out on the porch.

In the bedroom, after changing clothes, I turned on the hot tub in case the girls wanted to use it tomorrow. Feeling cooler, I went back to the porch where I found my warm beer sitting in the holder. Picking it up, I took a swig, then sat to drink it anyway.

A slight breeze began blowing off the lake, across the porch, which made the air a little more comfortable.   The peace and tranquility were something I had been missing.

Just before going to bed, I used the hot tub.   Not turning on the lights, I sat in the dark looking at lights from across the lake give off eerie shadows on the water.   It wasn't long before the toils of the day began to take their toll on me.

Standing by the open window, I let the cool night breeze cool me down before climbing into bed and falling asleep.

FIFTY-NINE

Saturday morning, I awoke after a good night's sleep, ready to begin the new day. The bed had been very comfortable, and the room still smelled new. Dressing in shorts and a T-shirt, I went downstairs to make a pot of coffee. Just as I was about to pour a cup, the phone rang.

"Hello," I said, answering.

"Are you hungry?"

"Yes, I just got up, is this Miranda?"

"Were you expecting someone else?"

"How did you get this number?"

"Knowing your name makes it sort of easy," she teased.

"Where would you like to go?" I asked.

"Nowhere. Phyllis and I will be making breakfast for the three of us as soon as we get there."

"You sure are a nice surprise," I said.

"I'm full of surprises," she said.

Fifteen minutes later, a car pulled in behind the house. Rushing out, before they could get out of their car, I took some of the food they were carrying. Then, with a bow, I ushered them into the house.

"Oh, this is so beautiful," Phyllis said.

"Yes. A girl could get used to living in a place like this," Miranda said.

Looking at the girls, I asked, "Are you two sisters or related in any way?"

Laughing, Miranda said, "No, just great friends."

"You could have fooled me."

"That is what most people think," Phyllis said.

We entered the back door that led to the kitchen. There, the girls stopped to gaze around.

"Seeing we are already in the kitchen," Miranda said, "go do what you like to do while we cook."

"Wouldn't you like to see the rest of the house first?" I asked.

"Yes, we would," Phyllis said.

"Then follow me," I told them.

As we began climbing the stairs to the second floor, we stopped midway.

"I see we have an alarm system built in," Phyllis quipped.

"There isn't any system," I told them.

"We just stepped on it," Phyllis chuckled.

"Oh yeah, I never thought of the stairs being an alarm," I chuckled, "I guess it would let me know if someone was trying to sneak up on me."

Reaching the second floor, I first took them into the master bedroom, then into the hot tub room. From there, I took them to see the two other bedrooms plus the bathroom.

"What kind of a weapon would you use if someone uninvited does come up the stairs?" Miranda asked.

"I never thought about that before, but if you girls will feel safer with a weapon, you girl can use whatever you use now."

"We have guns."

"Are they registered?"

"Of course, they are," Miranda said.

"Then there isn't a problem, and let me add one more thing. You girls are welcome to come here any time you want to feed me."

"Just if we feed you?" Phyllis teased.

"Now I can see how you two get along so well," I chuckled.

"I told Phyllis you love to tease," Miranda chuckled.

"I've never met two women who made me feel like the two of you do. There is something about the two of you that makes me trust you."

"How much do you trust us?" Phyllis asked.

"To show you how I feel, I will give you a key to this place and trust you won't hold parties here while I'm gone."

"Where are you going?" Phyllis asked.

By then, we were back on the first floor. The girls went back to the kitchen.

"I'm still in the military," I told them, "With five more years before I can retire. I'd like to have someone living here I can trust."

"You're willing to trust us to watch over this place while you're gone?"

"Yes."

"You actually just met us," Phyllis said, "How can you tell our personalities so quickly?"

"The way you girls look, the way you handle yourselves and the way you communicate tells me a lot about a person."

"You can trust us," Miranda said.

"If the two of you want, you can live here.   Then I won't have to worry about renters."

"How much a month?" Miranda asked.

"What are you paying now?" I asked.

"We split one thousand dollars rent, plus utilities."

"If you decide to live here, the only thing you will have to pay is the utilities.   Free rent is for keeping this place clean and safe."

"We'll do it," they quickly said, "And we will use the other two bedrooms for ourselves, as long as we can use the tub.   Your room will be for you when you come home to visit."

"The place will be yours.   Live in it as you wish."

"When can we move in?" Miranda asked.

"Today, if you want."

The girls began singing as they prepared breakfast.   While they were cooking, I took the opportunity to visit the shed.   Seeing the boat, I decided to put it in the water.

"Breakfast is ready," Miranda hollered.

Entering the house, I saw they had already set the table, and the steaming hot food was being placed on the table.   Gathering around the table, the girls held out their hands.   Taking their hands, I bowed my head.

"Thank you, Lord, for giving us this nice person and the new life he will afford us.   May this be a good relationship.   Amen."

"Thank you, Lord," I said, "For letting me bump into this beautiful creature and meeting her best friend."

We all squeezed hands, then sat to eat.   The food was absolutely delicious.

"Maybe I should reconsider what I said," I smiled.

When they stopped eating and looked at me, I began to laugh.

"If you cook like this, I'll quickly get out of shape."

"You had us scare for a moment," Miranda chuckled, then said, "Don't worry, you can cook for yourself."

Phyllis broke out in laughter.

"No," he said, "Your cooking is part of the deal. After all, it will be just once or twice a year. Now, one more thing."

"Oh, are we going to be slaves now?" Phyllis asked.

"Just when I need your help for things you will enjoy."

"Oh, well, that is different. What do you need?"

"There is a boat in the shed. Help me get it out and into the water, and it will be there for you to use."

Movement to the door was quick. I stood in shock watching them run to the door.

"Are you coming?" Miranda said, "This is your idea."

"Now I can see why you two aren't married."

"Why?" they asked, facing me.

"The two of you would drive a man crazy."

"Only if he was crazy with us to begin with," Miranda said.

"Do you two always back each other up?"

"Always."

"Even if you are wrong?"

"We are never wrong," Miranda said.

"Okay," I said, raising my hands in surrender, "I can see I would never win, so I'll just keep my mouth shut."

They laughed. Ten minutes later, we had the boat in the water and tied to the dock. The day was fun. Later that night, with my help, the girls had moved in. Instantly, the atmosphere in the home changed. I showed them how to light a fire, for cold nights and where to find the wood. The next day, I called to get extra wood delivered to the house.

After breakfast, we went for a swim. Seeing the girls in their two-piece bathing suits only heightened my desire for them. As much as I would like to bed either of them, I wasn't going to push the issue.

The remainder of my time home with the girls, we acted as one big family. We did everything together. In our spare time, we fished, swam and went out to dinner. Before bed, we used the hot tub. My time for staying home was quickly running out. Before I knew it, I was due back with my unit. The girls took me to the airport and hugged me. I saw them crying as I walked down the hall to board the plane. Leaving them was like tearing my heart out.

SIXTY

I t didn't take me long to get back into the flow of things. Meeting and spending all my time with the girls had given me a new lease of life. I received letters from both girls three times a week. They sent pictures of themselves and kept me up to date with what was going on. One of the first pictures showing snow, a few feet deep, had me worried. I called them.

"Hello," the voice said.

"Who is this?" I asked.

"Who is this?" she asked back.

"I'm sorry, I should have asked whom am I talking too."

"This is Miranda. Is this Bruce?"

"Yes."

"Is something wrong?"

"Not with me, but seeing the picture you sent after the storm had me wondering."

"There is nothing to worry about. Because of the angle of the roof, the snow couldn't gather there. The most difficult part was finding the sidewalk and driveway."

"I'm glad to hear that. Is the house warm enough?"

"God, yes. The house is so nicely insulated. We hardly ever have to use the heater. The fireplace gives us all the heat we need."

"I miss you guys," I said.

"We miss you, too, Bruce. If you were here, things would be a lot cozier."

"In what way?"

"We would have a man to harass and keep us sane."

"I know about the harassing part, but sane? Neither of you two are sane when it comes to me."

"That is because you ask for it."

"Do you have a boyfriend yet?"

"No. I'm happy the way things are."

"Don't you want a family?"

"Some day when I meet the guy I can't live without."

"What about Phyllis?"

"Oh, she has a boyfriend. I don't think it is serious, yet, but she does date."

"Maybe if I were there, you could go out with me now and then."

"Are you fishing or do you mean it?"

"Miranda, if I were there, I would be after you, not Phyllis, only you."

"You flatter me."

"You are worth all the flattery I can give you."

"Look, I hate to cut this short, but I have something on the stove. And don't worry, everything is great here."

"Goodbye, Miranda."

"Not goodbye, just so long for now," she said.

After hanging up, I realized how much I missed Miranda. I could picture her lounging on the couch or in her bathing suit. Someday, I would love to see her without clothes.

I didn't mention I was going on deployment tomorrow. Heading to Okinawa would normally be exciting, but my heart already belonged to someone else. The terrible part, I didn't know how she really felt about me. I hoped I wasn't in for another hurt. Maybe the ten-year difference in our age was too much for her.

At the end of the tour, I flew home. Miranda met me at the airport. As if it were the normal thing to do, I took her into my arms for a hug.

"Welcome home," she said.

The hug I received in return was stronger than I thought I would get. Liking the feel of her, I held on to her and looked into her eyes. Her eyes were glassy.

"Now that is what I call a great reception," I said.

"I liked how it felt, too," she said.

With our arms around each other, we made our way to collect my luggage. The way she kept in contact with me made me feel giddy with excitement.

"Where is Phyllis?" I asked.

"She is with her fiancée," Miranda said.

"She got engaged?"

"That is usually what happens when a girl gets a fiancée."

"Is she leaving you alone?"

"No. They don't live together. In fact, I think she is still a virgin."

"Good for her," I uttered.

With my luggage in hand, we made our way out the door. It was quite a walk to where she had parked her car. Nevertheless, just being with her made me forget about my pain. Every time I am near her, my heart beats wildly. Away from her, I felt lost and alone.

"How long are you home for this time?" she asked.

"A month. Any less time would be too short."

At the car, after I put my bag in the trunk and turned. Miranda was there with her arms extended. She wanted me to give her another hug. Was this her way of showing me how much she missed me? Holding her closeness like I was made, my heart skipped a beat. Not knowing how she really felt about me, I was afraid to say what I was feeling. Her hugs and greeting had given me hope, but I wanted to be sure how she felt before I opened up to her.

"Phyllis knows I came to get you," Miranda said, "Michael, her fiancée, is with her, waiting to meet you."

"Why does Phyllis want me to meet him?"

"I think she wants to know what you think. Women always wonder what other men think of their men."

"Just knowing you and Phyllis, I know they guy has to be good. I doubt either of you would ever date someone who isn't nice."

"How is it you always know what to say to make a woman feel special?"

"Because you are special to me."

"Can I ask you a personal question?"

"Of course."

"When you say I am special, how special am I to you?"

"Do you want me to open up?"

"Yes."

"Okay," I said, "I hope you won't think less of me for what I am about to say."

"I doubt I could think less of you for any reason."

"Honestly, since I met you, I haven't thought about any woman but you. I know this is putting you in a bad situation, but you asked, and I can't lie to you."

"Are you saying what I think you are saying?"

"I'm saying, I feel very deeply for you, but I haven't said my true feelings because I didn't want to make you feel uncomfortable."

"My God," she said, "If I had known how you felt, I would have acted differently myself."

"Whoa, am I dreaming?"

Pulling over to the side of the road, Miranda turned to face me. Her eyes were wide. That beautiful smile was covering her face, and tears were forming in her eyes.

"Do you feel for me what I feel for you?" I asked.

"If you are saying you love me, then yes, I feel for you how you feel for me."

Opening my arms, Miranda slid into them. Our lips met softly and tenderly. The tenderness of our kiss didn't last long. Almost instantly, a passion grew between us.   Our kisses quickly became heated. Breaking the kiss, I looked at her and said, "God, let's get home before things get out of hand."

"Phyllis and Michael will be there."

"If I'm right, they won't be there very long."

"Why not?"

"The look on our faces is going to tell them to get lost."

"I'm a virgin, Bruce."

"I didn't think otherwise."

The moment we pulled into the parking space, we were unable to control our emotions. Going into another clench, our lips were burning with need. Before we could break the kiss, Phyllis was knocking on the window.

"Hey, you two, come up for air?"

The man holding Phyllis was trying to pull her away from the car.

"Christ, Phyl, leave them alone."

"No, that is okay," I said.

Opening the door, I got out of the car. Immediately, Phyllis gave me a hug while Miranda was hugging Michael.

"Are you too?" Phyllis asked.

"What does it look like, Phyl?" Miranda said.

"I had a feeling how you felt after Bruce left last summer."

"Was I that obvious?"

"Hell yes," Phyllis said, "I have never seen you so confused or taken back as you were after he left. Why didn't you tell him how you felt? You have never had trouble telling people your feelings before."

"I didn't want to be to open in case he didn't feel the same way about me," Miranda said.

"Then how did those feelings get out this time?" Phyllis asked.

"It was a combination of honesty between us. I might have started the conversation, but I'm glad it is in the open," I said.

"Maybe Michael and I should stay somewhere else tonight?"

"No, we aren't going to do anything," I told her, "She is a virgin and wants to remain that way until after the wedding."

"Wedding? Are you?"

"Yes, I am."

Getting on one knee, I looked her in the eyes.

SIXTY-ONE

"Miranda, I don't have a ring for you, but if you say yes, you will get the ring first thing tomorrow when the store opens."

"Yes, yes, yes, I will marry you," Miranda cried.

"Great, but we won't marry until next year after you have graduate."

"Do I have to wait that long?"

"Don't you want to finish school?"

"Oh, I'll finish school. I just don't want to wait any longer to lose my virginity."

"Wholly crap," Phyllis cried, "How romantic."

"Are you sure, Miranda?"

"From tonight on, I want you to call me by my nickname, Randi."

"Okay, Randi, it is."

Seconds later, Randi was in my arms, kissing me."

"Phyl, why don't you and I get lost?" Michael said.

"Hell, if they are going to do it, why don't you and I celebrate our engagement too?" Phyllis said.

"Are you sure?" Mike asked.

"I've never been surer of myself as I am right now," Phyllis said.

Grabbing Michael's hand, she pulled him toward the car.   Seconds later, they were driving away.

"Now that they are gone," Miranda said, "I want you to make me into a true woman."

Holding hands, we made our way up the stairs to the bedroom.   In a hurry yet not wanting to be too fast, we slowly tantalized each other with a slow undress.

"I finally get to see the woman I love naked for the first time.   I have dreamed of this moment."

Her eyes clouded over with tears.

"I've never been naked in front of a man before," she uttered.

"My God, you're so gorgeous," I moaned.

Wiping her eyes, she dropped them to my groin.   They widened in surprise.

"Holly Crap, I didn't know erections were so big.   I've seen pictures, but they weren't this big."

Stepping to him, she reached for his hardness.

"Can I?" she asked.

"Of course," I answered.

"How can something be so big, so hard and yet feel so soft to the touch at the same time?"

"Miranda, oh, I'm sorry, I mean Randi.   We have to take our time with this.   Your gift to me means to much just to do it quickly.   You need to be loved, stimulated and crying for it before I do what you want me to do."

"Christ, I don't want to wait," she cried, "I've waited twenty-three years to lose my virginity and I want it gone."

"Go slow, Randi, the slower the better."

Pulling down the covers, I laid her down. Her golden hair spread across the pillow; her eyes stared into mine.

"I guess this is the time to say the words, 'I'm in love with you, Miranda."

Grabbing my shoulders, she pulled me down to cover her body.

"I love you, too, Bruce, I'm wild about you."

Feeling her plush body against mine made it difficult for me not to take her right then. As much as I wanted and needed her, I had to hold myself in check.

Rising from her, I moved onto the bed to kneel between her thighs. To my surprise, her hand quickly grasped me.

"Not yet," I moaned.

Right away, I began kissing her neck, then worked my way down to her plentiful breasts. Those cherry red nipples tasted good in my mouth. As I sucked a nipple, my other hand went down to cup her mound.

"Ooooh my Gooood, I'm, oh God, I'm," then she screamed as her body went taut.

After loving her breasts, I slowly kissed my way downward. Sliding my hands beneath her soft, round butt cheeks, I lifted her hips from the bed. Placing my lips against her virginal opening, I began to lick.

As if her body had an electrical charge flowing through it, her body went taut. Climax number two overtook her. Dropping her butt to the bed, I placed her legs over my shoulders, then kissed my way up her body to her breasts again. As soon as I nipped her nipple, she screamed for the third time.

"Now, damn you, stop teasing", she cried.

Her hand found me again. This time, she held my hardness against her wet opening. With her hips tilted upward, she encircled my waist with her arms and legs. With a squeeze, I felt the head of my erection begin to slide inside.

"Oh shit," she cried, "Take me now."

Grasping the soft cheeks of her round butt, I thrust a little harder.

I sank a little deeper.   When I met her maidenhead, I knew this was the part I had to be tender with.   With a couple of short thrusts, I was able to break her maiden head.

 "Oh God," she cried.

Stopping, I waited."

"You did it, now finish," she cried.

With that, I gave a final thrust.   She screamed.   Once again, I held still to let her adjust.   After a few seconds, she began pumping her hips. Her arms and legs, still encircling my body, tightened on me.

"I'm going to come, Randi and I'm not protected."

"I don't care, I want to feel you cum inside me."

"You could get pregnant."

"Unless you don't want children, now would be a good time to start, don't you think?"

"I thought you would want to be married before having children."

"That was the plan, but it's too late.   Empty inside me, Bruce."

With one hard last thrust, I began to empty inside her.   Feeling my ejaculation, she screamed a fourth time.   Sated and exhausted, we lay entwined to bask in the aftermath of pure pleasure.

"God, Bruce, I never knew."

"You have just showed me," I said, "I have found my true love."

"Me too," she said.

Throughout the night, we made love several times, not waking until noon the next day.

"Wholly crap," Miranda said, standing, "I'm so sore."

"It won't be so bad next time," I told her.

"I don't care how sore I get, now that I've had you, there is no way I can do without."

"Randi, you will have to go without it while I'm gone."

"I'm going with you."

"We don't have time to get married."

"Getting married can wait until next year," she said, "I'm going with you."

"I'll be gone nine months; wouldn't you prefer to be home with your parents?"

"When do you leave again?"

"In four months."

"If I stay here, you will be gone thirteen months before I see you again. Nine months is bad enough. I'm not giving up those three months before you go."

"What about your parents?"

"My dad is dead. Mom has remarried, and we haven't spoken in months. My sister, well, she and I never got along. Maybe now things will be different. Because of you, I feel like a different person."

SIXTY-TWO

"When will I get to meet your mother and stepfather?"

"Why don't we plan the wedding for next June when you get home.   It will give me time to get back with my family.   I'm going with you now, so don't even think about arguing.   When you deploy, I promise to go home and try mending fences with my family."

"As much as I love this place and would like to stay here my whole vacation," I said, "I think it best we go back now.   I need to find a place for us to live."

"Let me tell Phyllis what our plans are."

"Speaking of Phyllis, while we are gone, tell her she and Michael can live here."

"You would let Michael stay with her?"

"Why not?"

"What would you say for a double wedding?" Miranda asked, "If I can get back with my family, I would like to have the double wedding at the ranch."

"Ranch?   I didn't know you were a farm girl."

"I never considered myself a farm girl.   That is why I went to Teachers College."

"Speaking of teaching, do you plan on working your career?"

"Yes, until you get me pregnant."

"Hell, you might already be pregnant after last night."

"I don't care."

"How many kids do you want?" I asked.

"Two, a boy and a girl,' she said.

The next day, Phyllis came to the house with Michael in tow. With them there, I went over our plans.

"There has to be one other stipulation to agree on before we decide," Michael said.

"What is that?" I asked.

"Your bed is your bed. Phil and I will stay in our room. Your room will remain ready for the two of you when you come home."

"If that is the way you want it, I agree."

"Now that we agree, let me say both Phyllis and I are stunned you asked us to stay on. But there is one other thing. You have to give us a price on the rent. We don't want any gifts other than what you are giving us now."

"I'll tell you what. Before we leave, we will have a bank account set up for you. Put what you can afford into the savings."

"Okay. That will work," Michael said.

Later that night, while the four sat in the hot tub, Phyllis aired her concern.

"Are you sure about what you are going to be doing, Randi?" Phyllis asked.

"I've never been surer of myself as I am right now. In three months, when I come home, be prepared for me to move back in."

"I normally wouldn't say something like this, because I know you, but you being more like my sister, I feel more protective to you," Phyllis said, "So please don't hurt her. If you do, you will have to answer to me."

"I appreciate you saying this, Phyllis. When she does come home, I know she will be in good hands until I come home again."

"Then we are on the same page," Phyllis said.

"We are on the same page. You are the best friend any girl could have."

"Thank you for saying that, but remember what I said."

"Phyl, Bruce isn't going to hurt me, so stop worrying. We have a good, tight relationship that will last forever."

The girls hugged, then kissed as girls do, then sat back.

Early the next morning, Miranda and I went to the agency to tell them what I had planned. Despite what I had done, I wanted the agency to keep vigilance on the place, just in case.

"Don't you thrust Phyllis?"

"Of course, I do. If I didn't, I wouldn't let them stay there."

"Then why did you keep the agency as a lookout?"

"It doesn't hurt to be doubly safe. If something were to happen to Mike and Phyl, I'd like someone to tell me."

"Okay, now I understand."

"Are you upset by my actions?"

"Not now, I'm not. In fact, I think what you are doing makes good sense."

When Miranda and I got back to the house, I called the airport to book our flights. With only two more weeks of vacation left, going back this early to get Miranda settled was a good idea.

"Our flight time will be at ten o'clock tomorrow morning," I announced.

"Then we had better get packed," Miranda said.

"Aren't you going to call your parents?"

"No, I'll tell them when I get home," she said.

"When you get back home, why don't you plan our wedding?"

"We will."

"We?"

"Yes, since Phyllis and I want to marry on the same day, she and I will plan a double wedding."

"Did you know of their plans, Mike?"

"I knew they would be planning for the weddings, but I didn't know they wanted a double wedding."

"What is your idea about that?" I asked.

The girls sat listening to the conversation without saying a word.

"Sure. I'm for anything that will make Phyllis happy."

"Well put," I said.

"What Randi wants is what Randi gets," Mike said, "Having the four of us getting married together the same day would be great."

"I agree," I said.

"Now that you guys have told us what we already knew would happen, we both have to congratulate you on your fortitude," Miranda said.

Everyone broke into laughter.

Once the day was over, the four were back in the hot tub, relaxing together for the last time this year.

SIXTY-THREE

Early the next morning, Mike and Phyllis drove Miranda and I to the airport.

"I'm going to miss you, Randi," Phyllis cried, "but have a good life and hurry home."

"I am so happy, Phyl, I can't explain it, yet leaving you behind does bring on some sadness.   Having been friends for as long as we have, always left a void."

"And we will always remain friends," Phyllis said, wiping tears, "I will write and call once in a while."

"I will do the same," Miranda sobbed.

"Hey, look," I said, "If you two can get away, come out for a visit. We would love to have you.

"Honey," Randi said endearingly, "I will be coming home in three months."

"It's just an option," I said.

With a long drive back to home before them, Miranda and Phyllis hugged and kissed.   Mike and I shook hands.   A good friendship had developed.   Already missing our friends, a quietness came over them for a while.   On the plane, Miranda sat as close to me as she could get. Holding her hand helped her relax a little.

"I love you, Bruce," Randi said.

Turning to her with a smile, I kissed her softly, then, squeezing her hand, I told her how I felt, too.

"I love you, too, Randi. More than you will ever know," I told her, staring into her eyes, "I have never told that to any woman before."

Randi dabbed the tears from her eyes.

"I have never felt so happy and loved in my life," she sobbed

When the plane was finally in the air, I held her hand as she slept. Laying her head on my shoulder, Randi tightened her hand on mine, smiled, then closed her eyes.

The captain announcing the plane was about to land woke us from our nap. Feeling the descent, Randi clung tightly to my arm. The moment

the wheels touched down Randi let out a deep breath.

Emerging from the plane, we gathered our luggage. Leaving Miranda with the luggage, I went for the car. Moments later, I pulled up in front of the terminal. Getting out of the car, I helped Miranda into the car, then loaded the trunk.

"This is so different," Miranda said, "I didn't have any idea, except what I saw in pictures, what California was like."

I drove to Malibu, where I stopped at the restaurant on the pier overlooking the ocean.

"Where are we going to be living?"

"We still have sixty miles to go before we get to the base. We will stay in my apartment for the time I have here. Next year, when I get home, we will get married. I'll have to make two more deployments, then I should be up for shore duty for my last two years. When I retire, we can move back here, or if you prefer, remain there."

"Honey, I'll stay wherever you want. All I want is to be with you and our children."

"Are you going to start your career?"

"When I get home, I will put in for a substitute until you retire and we settle down.   Meanwhile, I can take more classes to get a higher degree."

"You're already smarter than I am," I told her.

"Maybe just in teaching," she said, "but you can teach me a lot about life in general."

It was getting late in the evening when I pulled into his parking space at the apartments.   Taking her hand, we walked into the compound.

"Look at that pool," she said.

"There will be plenty of time to enjoy it when you feel up to it."

"Tonight, I just want to go to bed."

"Are you that tired?"

The look she gave me told me it wasn't sleep she wanted.   Once in bed, Randi acted as if we hadn't had sex in weeks.   Even early in the morning, she was at me again, after which she made breakfast.

"Get out of bed, lazy head," she teased

"You wore me out last night," I told her.

She laughed.

"I hope you have more stamina than this," she teased.

"Come back to bed and I'll show you stamina."

"Ooooh, I hit a soft spot."

"Not really, I'm just trying to build up some energy so you will cry for me to stop."

"That will never happen.   Since I have had a taste of sex with you, there isn't anything that can stop my need."

"I hope that need doesn't take over while I'm gone," I said.

"That will never happen either, wise guy. Only one man is ever going to have me, and I have him already."

"Turn off the stove," I told her, "You have made me horny."

"Oh no," she said, "the food is ready. You only get desert when breakfast is over."

"Damn," I groaned.

Two hours later, Miranda and I were basking in the pool.

"Now, this is the life," Miranda said, "Good food, great sex and extreme comfort."

"I agree with everything you just said," I said.

"Are you going to show me around?"

"As soon as we get dressed," I told her.

"Let me get dressed first," she said.

"Are you already tired of showing me your body?"

"No. If we dress at the same time, we would never make it out of the bedroom."

"Oh, you don't need it much anymore, huh?"

"I will always be in the mood for you, just not when we want to go somewhere."

"I'm going to give you five minutes. If you're not ready when I get there, we are going to get a late start."

"In that case, to save time, let's go together."

Grabbing hands, we rushed to the apartment. Two hours later, we were on our way to the base.

"God, I have to be pregnant," she said.

"I don't know. As much as we go at each other, my sperm count could be too low."

We spent the day going around the base to give her an idea of where she could do her shopping. This time around, I would have to be with her, but once we were married, she would be on her own. Leaving the base, I drove to the ocean. We walked the beach and visited the pier to see how the fishing was. From there, we had a late lunch.

"Show me what the housing is like around here. Maybe we can find a cheap rent."

I drove around. The houses we saw were either too run-down or too expensive. In the end, Miranda decided it would be best to stay in the apartment for the three months.

SIXTY-FOUR

MIRANDA

The day I met Bruce was a day I would never forget. When he banged into my cart, making me drop what I was holding, instant anger surged through me. The moment I looked into his eyes, my anger disappeared. Where did this man come from, I wondered? He's absolutely the perfect man I've been looking for. I wasn't looking for a man, but this accidental meeting changed my outlook.

As badly as I wanted to meet this man, I didn't have the guts to try. He did introduce himself, but that was the extent of our conversation. Leaving him without a word made me angry at myself. Then, analyzing the situation to make myself feel better, I tried to tell myself he was too old anyway. Nevertheless, as I walked each aisle, I couldn't get the guy out of my mind.

Then another chance gave me a second chance. As I was checking my goods, I found I didn't have enough money to pay. Not knowing the guy was standing behind me, I became totally embarrassed. To make matters worse, when the guy insisted on bailing me out, I didn't have the heart to argue.

After being bailed out, I walked a short distance away to wait for him. When the guy came from the cashier, I walked over to him.

"My names is Miranda; can I ask yours?"

"It's Bruce."

"That was very nice of you, Bruce," I said, "But you didn't have to do that."

"I know I didn't have to, but I wanted too," he said, smiling, "Just consider it as being helpful."

I liked his looks, his voice and the way he handled everything. Walking with him to the parking, I was surprised how close we parked near each other. Then the guy did something else that put me on edge. He asked me to lunch. I almost choked. When I didn't answer right away, he must have thought my answer would be no.

After giving an apology to the guy, he started to turn away. As he began unloading his goods, I realized I didn't want to miss this golden opportunity. Swallowing my fear, I went to him. His back is to me. When I placed my hand on his arm, he seemed startled. Surprise was etched on his face, but it quickly changed to a fantastic smile.

This time, when Bruce asked where a nice place to eat would be, I took advantage.

"I know the perfect place. Follow me."

As I drove, I kept looking in my rear-view mirror to be sure he was really following me. After a few miles around the lake, I pulled into a parking space by the cafe. Getting out of my car, I had to wait for him to find a spot. Then, with that fantastic smile on his face, he met me at the door. Opening the door, he allowed me to enter first. It was the first time in my life that a man treated me like a lady.

Inside, he looked around. A sign said Seat yourself. Seeing an empty table by the windows, he led the way. When we got to the table, I was about to pull out a chair when I was interrupted. The guy pulled my chair for me, then waited for her to get comfortable. Before pushing me in. I thought I was in heaven. When he turned to take his seat, I swooned. Holding her breath, I did the best I could to hold the tears. Once he was seated in front of me, I couldn't help staring into his beautiful green eyes.

"What would you like?" he asked.

I told him.   He ordered for me.   The whole time we were waiting for our food, I stared and smiled at him.   I couldn't believe I was with a guy who did everything for me.   He asked me about what I liked and listened tentatively to all my words.

As we ate, our conversation centered around who they were and what we did for a living.   He invited me and my roommate to see his home.   I had always wondered what the house looked like inside, since all the renovations had been done.   When lunch was over, he paid and then walked me to my car.   Again, he held the door for me and waited until I was settled.

Driving away, we drove in opposite directions.   Arriving back at my apartment, I told my roommate what had just happened and what I had planned.   Happy for me, Phyllis agreed to accompany me on my adventure tomorrow.

Saturday morning, I was feeling overly excited when I banged on Phyllis's bedroom door.   Once she was up and organized, I drove to where I knew the guy was living.   Fifteen minutes later, I pulled in next to where his car was parked.

Before I could get out of my car, Bruce came running from the house. To help me out of the car, then turning, he faced Phyllis.   Taking the food from our hands, he ushered us into the house.   Once inside, Bruce took us on a tour.   Reaching the second floor, he showed us the master bedroom

and the hot tub.   From there, he showed us the two other bedrooms and the bathroom.   After the tour, we went back to the kitchen.

When Bruce was ordered from the kitchen, he went outside.   A few moments later, when the food was ready, I called him in for breakfast. Coming into the house, he washed his hands at the kitchen sink.

Turning, he saw what us girls had done.   We were proud of our display.   We had set the table and had steaming hot food on the table. Standing by the table with our hands out, Bruce knew what we wanted. Taking our hands, we bowed our heads.   After I gave the grace, we shook hands and sat. From the expression on his face, Bruce wasn't surprised at how good the food tasted.   After the meal, he sat back in his chair to savor his satisfaction.

"How would you girls like to live here while I'm gone?"

"You would trust us?" Miranda asked.

"How much would we have to pay?"

"Rent would be free.   Utilities would be all you have to pay."

"Why would you offer free rent?" Phyllis asked.

"It would be my way of showing you my appreciation for you taking care of this place."

"How could we refuse?" we said in unison.

"Now that you have agreed, I need your help for things something you will enjoy."

"What do you need?"

"There is a boat in the shed.   Help me put it in the water, and it's yours to use."

Quickly moving to the door, we turned to look at him.

Ten minutes later, we had the boat in the water and tied to the dock. Later that night, Bruce helped us girls to move into our new bedrooms. The atmosphere in this home seemed to have changed.   He showed us girls how to light a fire for cold nights, then ordered a cord of wood to be delivered to the house.   After breakfast, the three of us went for a swim.   Seeing Bruce in his bathing suit, I instantly felt for him what I had never felt for any man.

For the remainder of his time at home with us girls, we acted as one big family.   We did everything together, we fished, swam, went out to dinner and used the hot tub every night.   Before he knew it, he was due back with his unit.   We girls took him to the airport, hugged him and cried at his departure.

SIXTY-FIVE

MIRANDA

Ten months later, I met Bruce at the airport. I was so happy to see him, I flung my arms around his neck to give him a strong hug. Feeling the strength of his arms surround me, I leaned back to look into his eyes.

Standing as close together as we were, with our arms around each other, we couldn't resist staring at each other. Both could see the desire to kiss, but neither wanted to be the first to initiate it. Breaking our contact, we made our way to get his luggage.

With his luggage in hand, he headed out the door. Being it was a long walk to where I had parked her car, I took a deep breath. The walk didn't bother me, it was my just being near him that made my heart beat wildly.

"How long are you home for this time?" I asked.

"A month. Any less time would be too short."

As soon as we reached the car, I couldn't contain myself any longer. Grabbing him, I turned him to face me. Again, I hugged him tightly, wanting to show him how much I really missed him. Feeling as if I were on cloud nine, I climbed into the car. As I drove off, I was so excited about him being home that I didn't know what to say, so I said the first thing that came to my mind.

"Phyllis knows I came to get you," she uttered, "She and Michael are waiting to meet you."

"Why does Phyllis want me to meet her fiancée?"

"I think she wants to know what you think. Women always wonder what other men thinks of their men."

"Just knowing you and Phyllis, I know the guy will be good. I doubt either of you would pick someone who wasn't nice."

"How is it you always say thing that make me feel special?"

"Because to me, you are special."

"Can I ask you a personal question?"

"Of course."

"When you say I am special, how special am I to you?"

Bruce opened up to her. To his surprise, she had the same feeling for him. After hearing his words, I was unable to drive any further. Pulling over to the side of the road, I dried my eyes, then, turning to face him, I looked deep into his eyes. His eyes were wide and cloudy. A smile covered his face.

After venting our feelings for each other, I quickly slid into his open arms. Our lips met for the first time in a kiss that was soft and tender. Our tenderness didn't last long. Almost instantly, the passion we were feeling grew hot between us. Breaking the kiss, Bruce said, "God, let's get home before things get out of hand."

"Phyllis and Michael will be there."

"If I'm right, they won't be there very long."

"Why not?"

"The look on our faces is going to tell them to get lost."

"I'm a virgin, Bruce."

"I didn't think otherwise."

Sucking in a huge deep breath, I turned my attention to the road. All hepper, my foot got a little heavy on the gas pedal. The moment I pulled into the parking space, we went into another clench.   Our lips burned with need.   Before we could break the kiss, Phyllis was knocking on the window.

"Hey, you two, come up for air?"

A man was trying to pull Phyllis away.

"Christ, Phyl, leave them alone."

Seeing the look on the guy's face, Bruce broke the kiss.

"No, that is okay," Bruce said.

Opening the car door, he climbed out of the car.   With Phyllis standing before him, he offered her a hug.   After the four of us hugged and shook hands, we continued the conversation.   It soon came to light how Bruce felt about me.   In that moment, Bruce put everything on the table.

Kneeling, Bruce said, "Would you do me the honor and marry?"

That was the clue that sent Phyllis and Michael away for the night.

As Bruce got to his feet, Miranda flung her arms around his neck. Her kiss was accentuated with her tongue entering his mouth.   When she broke the kiss, she stunned everyone.

"Great," she exclaimed, "Now, I won't have to wait to get married to lose my virginity."

"Don't you want to finish school?"

"Oh, I'll finish school.   I just don't want to wait that long to lose my virginity."

"Wholly crap," Phyllis cried, "How romantic."

"Are you sure, Miranda?"

"From tonight on, I want you to call me by my nickname, Randi."

"Okay, Randi, it is."

SIXTY-SIX

MIRANDA

"**T**hey are gone," I quickly said, "Now make me a woman."

Taking my hand, we made our way up the stairs to the bedroom. In a hurry, yet not wanting to be too fast, we undressed in a tantalizing speed.

"I've never been naked in front of a man before," I uttered.

"My God, you're so gorgeous," Bruce groaned.

My eyes dropped to his groin.

"Holly Crap, I didn't know erections were so big. I've seen pictures, but they weren't that big."

Stepping closer to him, I asked.

"Can I?"

"Of course."

Placing my hand on his hardness, I gasped.

"How can something be so big and so hard, yet feel so soft to the touch at the same time?"

"Miranda, oh, I'm sorry, I mean Randi. We have to take our time with this. Your gift to me means to much just to do it quickly. You need to be loved, stimulated and crying for it before I take your virginity."

"Christ, I don't want to wait," she cried, "I've waited twenty-three years to lose my virginity. Now, I want it gone."

"Go slow, Randi, the slower we go, the better it will be."

Pulling down the covers, Bruce waited for me to lay down. As I lowered my body to the bed, I let my golden hair spread across the pillow. Her eyes never left my face.

"I guess this is the time for me to say the words, 'I'm in love with you, Miranda Graham."

As Bruce slid onto the bed, I grabbed his shoulders to pull him down to cover her body.

"I love you too, Bruce Benson," I whispered, "I am so wild for you, I can't wait for this to happen."

Feeling his hard body coming down on me, she swooned. My need to feel him between my open thighs was overwhelming. I needed to feel of his hardness press against her womanhood. But he wouldn't let it happen. Swooning, I wrapped him tightly in my limbs. The moment he kissed my neck, I went wild. It wasn't long before Bruce was nibbling and licking my nipples. With a sensation I had never felt before, it made me scream. Then his hand was cupping my mound.

Feeling him kiss his way down my body was driving me crazy. When he slid his hands beneath my bottom and lifted my hips from the bed, I went with him. The moment Bruce kissed my virginal opening, pure pleasure shot through me, bringing me to an immediate second climax. Then, with my legs over his shoulders, he again began kissing his way up my body. Working my nipples again made me scream for the third time.

"Now, damn you," she cried.

Reaching between him, I quickly grasped him. This time, I held his hardness against my opening. Dropping my legs from his shoulders, I encircled his waist. The movement tilted my hips just enough to allow him to insert himself between the lips of my womanhood.

"Oh shit," she cried, "I can't believe this is happening."

Caught in my own fury, Bruce trusted a little harder.   I felt him hit my maidenhead. I knew I was up for pain.   Slowly, he worked me until I felt a sharp pain he broke through.   Now that the pain was over, his entry was easier.   As he slid deeper inch by inch, I shuddered with pleasure.   Eventually, his short thrusts finally completely filled me.   He now as all the way inside me.   Bruce held still, letting my body adjust to his invasion.   Taking a deep breath, I began thrusting my hips to match his thrusts.   With my arms and legs holding his body in place, I refused to release him when he warned me, he was about to climax.

Wanting his seed, I held in place.   Feeling him flood my insides, I screamed for the fourth time.   Totally satisfied, I kept him locked tightly to me as we basked in the aftermath of fantastic pleasure.

"God, Bruce, I never knew."

SIXTY-SEVEN

MIRANDA

The trip to California was magical for me. In my mind, I had it all. I have the man I love and the time to live with him, in a new place, even if it were for a short period of time. My only wish was not to have to go home in three months. I wanted to wait for my man to return right where I was, but nine months will seem like an eternity.

Getting off the plane in LAX, I found congestion ruled. The crowd coming and going was suffocating. It wasn't difficult to walk anywhere without being bumped into. The attitude of the people in California seemed to be, get out of my way, I was here first. I quickly thought, if I weren't with Bruce, I would hop on the next plane home.

In Oxnard, I found congestion wasn't as bad. The apartment he was living in was more than satisfying. I really didn't care where we lived as long as I was with the man I loved.

The next day, Bruce gave me a tour of the base and the surrounding towns. In our travels, I found the one town she could like. If they were staying longer than three months, we would have love to live in Camarillo.

"Once I retire, you will have to make a choice of where you want to live. There is the home by the lake or here in Camarillo. Whichever you want."

"Before you get home, I will have to get with my mother and sister to see if we can't become a closer family. My sister has a baby, and it's a shame we all can't get along. Maybe you can help me change things."

"I'll do the best I can, Randi."

The three months quickly went by. Before I knew it, Bruce was scheduled to deploy.

"Just think, in a little more than two years I will be retiring," he said, "Then all you have to do is make up your mind where you want to live."

"In two years, we could have two children."

"That is a possibility. Where do you think you and the kids would be the happiest?"

"I'm sort of leaning to home. We will be living at a lake, and the town is small and quiet."

The day Bruce was to deploy, I went to the airport with him. With a smile on my face, she said, "Hurry home."

"I'll be there as quickly as I can."

"The both of us will be waiting."

"Both of you?"

Taking his hand, I placed it on my belly.

"It is due in six months."

"Holly Christ, I'm going to be a daddy."

Hugging, we kissed one last time before he boarded the plane.

With the plane in the air and out of sight, IA wiped the tears from my eyes. I never felt so lonely. Sadly, I made my way to the car. Driving home from the base, I felt so lost and lonesome. Tomorrow I will be flying home to start a new way of living.

In the short time we were living together, we made some good friends. Those friends took me to the airport. They would keep our car in their yard for them until Bruce got home.

SIXTY-EIGHT

BRUCE

Nine months in Guam seemed like two years to me. Normally, being in any country somewhere never bothered me. I enjoyed getting to know the people, learning their ways and their languages. This time, even though I have been to Guam before, mentally I was in Connecticut.

News from home used to help make my trips a little easier to handle. This time, a few did help, but most only seemed to make the time go slower. I did get good news from Miranda.

Bruce, I miss you so terribly. Good news is, I made up with my mother and mended most of our differences. Sadly, there still seems to be some distance between my sister and me. As far as the baby is concerned, it won't be long before she arrives. Love for ever, Randi.

The news that Miranda was giving me a daughter made me happy, but knowing I wouldn't be there for my daughter's birth made me sad. I wanted to be there for Miranda. But it would be two more months before I got home.

Randi, I'm sorry I won't be there for the birth of our daughter, but I will be home in two months. This is the first time I ever went on deployment and didn't want to be here. You are my life now. In two years, I will be home forever. That will be when I can help you rear our daughter. Who knows, there might even be another child? You are the love of my heart. Bruce.

The next two months went by slowly. I received the news about my daughter being born. She should be almost two months old when I get to hold her for the first time. The day of the flight didn't seem to move quick enough. When the plane landed in Hueneme, I was on the next flight to Connecticut. Landing in Connecticut, I was met by Miranda. She wasn't holding our two-month-old daughter.

"Randi," I cried.

Dropping my bag, I crushed her in my arms. Our kisses were hungry.

"Bruce," she cried, clinging tightly to me.

"Where is April?" I asked.

"Mom is watching her. I wanted time alone with you."

"Do we go to the house first?"

"No, we go to the room I rented, not far from here."

"I can't wait to get you in bed," I told her.

"That was my thought exactly," she said, kissing me again.

Fifteen minutes later, we were in bed, making up for lost time. After a night of hot sex, I knew it was going to be a long drive home. It was early afternoon when they got to Miranda's mother's home. A few extra cars were parked along the street when I pulled up to the house.

Entering the house, the noise of the people came from the backyard. Miranda went into the backyard first.

"We're here, everyone," she announced.

Immediately, the noise stopped. When I stepped into the backyard, my heart stood still.

"Bruce?"

"Lana?"

"Do you two know each other?" Lana's husband asked.

"Yes. I don't know, seventeen years ago, I guess," Lana said.

"You haven't changed in all the years, Lana," I said.

It seemed everyone was waiting for an explanation.

"I had just come home on leave and was thumbing a ride to Madison, where my parents lived. It was stifling hot. If Lana hadn't stopped, I might have gotten heat stroke."

"Because he was in uniform, I stopped to give him ride. Since I was on my way to Clinton and it was around noon, we stopped for lunch where we had a lengthy conversation."

"Where were you when I called?" Miranda asked.

"I had just dropped him off at the restaurant outside the park.

"I told him I was married and had two daughters. It was a nice afternoon after that convention."

Then the subject changed.

"Where did you meet Miranda?" Lana asked.

"To be honest, I was shopping. I ran my cart into hers. It wasn't until later; we began talking and things escalated."

"Yes, and she was star-struck," Phyllis said.

"Phyllis," Randi cried, "I'm so glad you came. Where is Mike?"

"He is probably in the bathroom."

I quickly gave Phyllis a hug and a light kiss on the cheek.

Laughing, Miranda said, "The next morning, Phyllis and I went to his home to make breakfast. I'm glad we did since Phyllis and I got to live in his house free while he was gone."

"One of these days soon, I hope all of you will come to the house by the lake for a barbecue weekend."

Right about then, a young man around fourteen or fifteen came into the room.   Again, my heart stopped.   The young man had a slight resemblance to me.

"Brett, meet your uncle to be.   Bruce, this is my youngest child."

"Hello Brett.

His handshake was strong.   His eyes were the same color as mine.

"So, we meet again," a voice said.

"Henry?" I said shocked.

Gazing around, I saw Julia standing in the crowd.   Standing with her was my son, who had to be around ten.

"What are you doing here?" I asked.

"Julia is Miranda's older sister," Henry told me.

Julia stepped up to us.

"Hello, Bruce, this is Joshua."

"Hi Joshua, it is nice to meet you."

"Hold it," Miranda cut in, "How is it you know my sister?"

"I was stationed in Hueneme, and we lived in the same apartment as he did," Henry offered.

"Yes, and Bruce was a big help to me while Henry was overseas," Julia said.

"Bruce knows about Joshua," Henry said, "He gave Julia a gift for the baby while she was in the hospital having our son."

"Is that where we stayed?" Miranda asked.

"Yes."

"I used to think Bruce and Julia had a thing going."

"I kept telling him, Bruce, and we were just good friends."

SIXTY-NINE

The party didn't last long. People began drifting off. Feeling sick to my stomach from the stress, I stood off to the side to watch Miranda talk to her sister. Seeing Henry talking to Samuel didn't help. Heavy guilt weighed on me every time someone talked to someone else about the family.

"Bruce," Miranda said, "Isn't it time for us to go?"

"Okay, let me say goodbye to everyone."

Shaking hands with Mike and Henry, I then moved to hug Lana and Julia.

When I approached Lana, Julia left us alone. Embracing Lana, she said, continuing the hug, "I guess you can tell Brett is your child."

"Yes, he has a lot of my features."

"How did you get Henry to believe Joshua was his son?"

"You know about that, too?"

"He and Brett are brothers even though they have different mothers."

"I'm surprised the two of you don't hate me."

"As it turns out, my relationship and Julia's was all your fault. We both sort of seduced you."

Glancing at Randi, I saw her talking to her sister.

"Look, let's talk again. Randi wants to take off."

"I don't blame her.   If it were me, I would have you out of here hours ago."

I gave her a stare before walking away.

"Yes, I still have the hots for you," Lana whispered.

Making my way to where Miranda and Julia were talking, I was wondering what was going to happen.   When I reached them, Randi grabbed my arm.

"What were you and Mom talking about?"

"Just remembering the past."

"Which reminds me," Julia said, "I'd like to have a long talk with you too."

"Can't it wait until tomorrow?" Randi said, "I need to have some time along with for a while."

"Can we talk tomorrow, Bruce?"

"Will Henry be alright with that?"

"He is over you now," Julia said.

Randi listened to my exchange with Julia, but didn't say anything. Grabbing Randi, I made a beeline for the stairs leading to our room.

Upon entering our room, Randi quickly clung to me.

"Finally," she sighed, "I didn't think I would ever get you away from my mother or sister."

"It was a shock to know, I knew your mother and sister before I met you.   And I can now see the resemblance to the three of you."

"Tonight, you are mine. Tomorrow you can chat with both of them if you want.   Just remember who you are sleeping with."

"That I could never forget."

Having April in the room with us didn't let us get much sleep. Of course, we didn't have any trouble exhausting ourselves. During the night, I awoke when April needed to be fed and again when she needed changing.

Knowing Randi got less sleep than I did, I got up and took April with me so Randi could sleep. Going to the kitchen, I found Lana sipping on a cup of coffee.

"We have to talk," Lana whispered.

"About what?" I asked.

"The problem we are going to have when you retire."

"What sort of problem?"

"Family problems. Did Randi figure out you have two other children in this family?"

"I don't know. It shouldn't make a difference. Both of those children were conceived when I was single. Do the boys know I am their father?"

"No, neither Julia or I know how to tell them."

"Maybe we just leave it as it is."

"I'm forty-nine now. Thank God Brett will be gone in a couple years."

"Does your husband know the origin of the child?"

"No. If he did, I doubt he would stay with me."

"Why would he leave you. What you did before you married him should add into the equation."

"You are right, but some men are funny that way, especially since I was married when you got me pregnant."

"You don't know how much I agonized about that. By all rights, we should have never had sex."

"Your right about that, too, but my husband, at that time, didn't take care of my needs. I was too young to go without, and you were a horny sailor."

"And I don't regret our time together. I do feel guilty, but I will never regret our time together."

"Even after all these years, I still miss your love making."

"Lana, that part of our lives is over. I will be marrying your youngest daughter, and we already have a child. I love your daughter too much to cheat on her, even with you."

"I'm glad to hear you say that," Lana said, "but I also wish you didn't feel that way."

When April began to cry, Lana took charge. After changing her diaper, I took her back to bed. Randi was still sleeping soundly.

It was the same with Julia. How in the hell was I going to handle this family? Lana and I have spent a lot of time together. It was obvious we still had strong feelings for each other. Then Julia. That was a story all its own. Joshua is believed to be Henry's child, and that is the way Bruce hoped it would stay. What would happen if Miranda ever learned the truth about him and her mother, and her sister?

As time moved on, Bruce finished his time in the service. He retired and lived with Miranda, April and Benjamin.